KINSHU

AUTUMN BROCADE

KINSHU

AUTUMN BROCADE

Teru Miyamoto

Translated from the Japanese by Roger K. Thomas

A New Directions Book

This book has been selected by the Japanese Literature Publishing
Project (JLPP), which is run by the Japanese Literature Publishing and
Promotion Center (J-Lit Center) on behalf of the
Agency for Cultural Affairs of Japan.

Manufactured in the United States of America
New Directions Books are printed on acid-free paper.
First published clothbound by New Directions in 2005
Published simultaneously in Canada by Penguin Books Canada Limited
Book and jacket design: Lawrence Wolfson Design, NY

Library of Congress Cataloging-in-Publication Data

Miyamoto, Teru.
  [Kinshû. English]
  Autumn brocade = Kinshu / Teru Miyamoto ; translated from the
  Japanese by Roger K.Thomas.
    p. cm.
  ISBN 0-8112-1633-0 (alk. paper)
  I. Thomas, Roger K. II. Title. III. Title: Kinshu.
PL856.I8735K56 2005
895.6'35--dc22

                                                           2005020111

New Directions Books are published for James Laughlin
by New Directions Publishing Corporation
80 Eighth Avenue, New York, NY 10011

CONTENTS

KINSHU

AUTUMN BROCADE

Dear Yasuaki,

I never imagined I would run into you on Mount Zaô, in the gondola lift going from the dahlia garden to Dokko Pond. I was so surprised that I was speechless for the whole twenty-minute ride up the mountain.

It must be twelve or thirteen years since I last wrote you a letter. I thought I would never see you again, but then meeting you unexpectedly like that and noticing how much your face had changed and the look in your eyes... After much hesitation and deliberation, I tried every way I could to find out your address, and finally wrote you this letter. Please feel free to laugh at my capricious and impulsive nature, which remains the same as it always was.

That day, on the spur of the moment, I boarded the Tsubasa III express train from Ueno Station, intending to show my son the stars from the top of Mount Zaô. (His name is Kiyotaka, and he is eight years old.) You probably noticed when we were in the lift that Kiyotaka was born handicapped: not only is he paralyzed from the waist down but he is also two or three years behind in mental development compared with other children his age. Yet for some reason he is fond of stargazing, so much so that on clear nights he goes into the inner garden of our home in Kôroen and stares up at the sky, engrossed for hours on end. During our brief stay in Tokyo at my father's condominium in Aoyama, I was leafing through a magazine the evening before we were due to return to Kôroen when a photograph of the night sky taken from the summit of Mount Zaô caught my eye. The sight of the heavens studded with stars took my breath away, and I wondered if there might be some way to show the actual scene to Kiyotaka, who had never been on a long outing.

Father turned seventy this year, but he continues to show up hale and hearty at the company every day. What's more, in order to supervise the Tokyo branch office, he spends half of every month in the same Aoyama condominium you knew. Compared to ten years ago, his hair has turned completely white and he's a little stooped, but he manages to keep in good spirits. He divides his time equally between Kôroen and the Aoyama condominium.

Around the beginning of October, when the company car came to pick him up, he lost his footing going down the stone staircase in front of the condominium and injured his ankle badly—a hairline fracture and a good deal of swelling, which left him unable to walk. In a panic, I jumped on the Shinkansen bullet train with Kiyotaka and rushed to see him. No sooner had he lost his mobility than he became difficult to deal with. He disliked the fussy way Ikuko looked after him, and telephoned for me to come over though I had just left. Thinking that it might turn out to be a long stay, I had no choice but to take Kiyotaka along. As soon as Father saw our faces he calmed down. Perhaps worrying about the house in Kôroen, he perversely started to say that we should go back right away. I didn't know whether to be amazed or amused by his willfulness. Entrusting him to the care of Ikuko and Okabe, his secretary, I decided to return to Kôroen and left for Tokyo Station with Kiyotaka.

It was there that I saw a travel poster for Mount Zaô. The large photograph was filled with the spreading branches of brightly colored trees in autumn. I had always associated Zaô with its ice-covered trees in winter, and I stood in the Tokyo Station concourse imagining how these trees—which would become pillars of ice, but were now brilliant with autumn foliage—would look swaying in the breeze under a star-studded night sky. For some reason, I felt an irresistible urge to let my handicapped child experience the invigorating mountains and see all the stars. When I told Kiyotaka this, his eyes brightened and he begged me to take him there. Although it seemed too much of an adventure for the two of us, we went to a travel agent inside the station and bought train tickets to Yamagata. Then we made reservations at an inn at Zaô Hot Spring, and tried to reserve return seats on a flight from Sendai to Osaka Airport. No seats were available, though, and we had to change our plans and stay an extra night at either Zaô or Sendai before our return flight. I decided to stay two nights at Zaô, so we headed for Ueno Station to catch the train there. If we had stayed only one night at Zaô, I would not have run into you. It all seems very strange to me now.

Yamagata was cloudy. Feeling somewhat disappointed, I sat in the cab from Yamagata Station to Zaô Hot Spring and looked up at the sky. Suddenly I realized this was the second time I had visited this northeastern region. I remembered setting out for Towada from Lake Tazawa in Akita Prefecture on our honeymoon.

Kiyotaka and I stayed at the inn in the hot spring resort. The strong smell of sulfur made it difficult to breathe, and the overflowing hot water was running down channels on both sides of the street. Clouds covered the night sky, without a sliver of moon or any stars visible, but the mountain air was bracing. For the first time my son and I were on a trip, and we were in a buoyant mood. The next morning it was clear. Holding his crutches in front of him, Kiyotaka didn't want to waste a minute getting to the gondola, so immediately after breakfast we set off for the gondola platform in the dahlia garden. To think that we should board the same gondola halfway up Mount Zaô at the same time as you— one of countless gondolas going up and down the mountain in such an out-of-the-way place as Yamagata! It sends a shiver down my spine just to think about such a coincidence.

Several groups of people were waiting to get on the lift, but after two or three minutes we boarded. The attendant opened the gondola door, lifted Kiyotaka and his crutches, and set him inside. Then I got on. I heard the attendant announce that he could take one more, and a man in a light brown coat boarded the cramped gondola and sat down opposite us. The door closed, and the moment the lift lurched forward I realized it was you. How can I begin to express my astonishment? You were not yet aware of me and were gazing at the scenery with your chin buried in the upturned collar of your coat. While you were absently looking out of the window, I kept staring at your face, never blinking once. I had got on the gondola to see the beautiful autumn leaves, but I didn't give the trees a glance; I just fixed my eyes on the man in front of me.

During those few minutes, the question kept racing through my mind whether or not this person could actually be Arima Yasuaki, my former husband. And if it was Arima Yasuaki, why was he riding this gondola on Mount Zaô in Yamagata? It wasn't just my surprise at this incredible coincidence; your face looked totally different from the one that was etched in my memory. Ten years... I had been twenty-five years old then, and I'm thirty-five now, so you must be thirty-seven. Both of us have reached the stage when the effects of age begin to show on the face. Even so, the change in your appearance was severe, and I understood that you had definitely not had an easy time. Please don't take offense. I myself don't really understand why I'm writing a letter like this. I just want to put down my side of things—something I'll probably never do again—and describe exactly how I feel. Yet, in spite of my writing to you like this, I still haven't decided whether I'll actually post my letter or not.

At length you glanced in my direction, then turned again to the scenery outside the window. Then you looked at me once more, your eyes wide with amazement. It seems as if we stared at each other for an eternity. I thought I should say something, but words failed me. I finally managed to say, "It's been a long time, hasn't it?" After responding, "Yes, it has," you looked at Kiyotaka with a blank expression and asked, "Is this your boy?" It was all I

5

could do to answer in the affirmative, in a voice that was almost trembling.

The clusters of trees with scarlet leaves flowing past both sides of the gondola were reflected indifferently in my eyes. How often have I been asked, "Is this your boy?" When Kiyotaka was smaller, with disabled limbs and a face that clearly revealed his mental retardation, some people would ask the question with an obvious look of pity, while others would contrive a sort of vacuity. Each time I would muster all my energy, look the person straight in the eye, and proudly answer, "Yes." Yet when you asked, "Is this your boy?" I was overcome by shame of a sort I had never experienced before, and replied hesitantly, in a weak voice.

The gondola proceeded slowly up the mountain toward the landing platform by Dokko Pond. The Asahi Range was coming into view in the distance, while in a fold in the mountain below, the roofs of buildings in the resort town were minuscule points of reflected light. On the mountain slope, the lone red roof of a hotel, set apart from the others, appeared intermittently through gaps in the trees. I distinctly recall even now that for some reason it reminded me of a scroll painting from the Kamakura period depicting the flames of hell. Why did it make me think of something like that? Perhaps my nervousness and mental agitation had put me in a strange state of mind as the gondola swayed along. I should have been able to talk about all sorts of things with you during the twenty-minute ride, but I just sat in stony silence, thinking only of how soon we could arrive before I could get off. It was exactly the same as when we parted ten years ago. At that time, we really needed to discuss our feelings about the divorce openly, yet we did not. Ten years ago I stubbornly refused to force you to explain the incident, and you kept your perverse silence, not offering even a word of excuse. Being twenty-five at the time, gentleness and forbearance were not in my nature. You were twenty-seven, and had sunk as low as you could.

When the trees outside the gondola became denser, blocking the sunlight and darkening the inside, you looked straight ahead over my shoulder, and muttered, "We're here now." In that instant, I saw the scar on the right side of your neck. "Ah, that's from the wound back then," I thought, and hurriedly looked away. We got off at the dirty, gray landing stage and, standing on the winding path to Dokko Pond, you said with a slight bow, "Well, goodbye then," and walked briskly away.

I'll be as candid as possible in this letter. For a while after you disappeared, I stood there glued to the spot. It seemed as if we were parting for good, and I had to fight the urge to burst into tears. Why did such a feeling come over me? I hardly understand myself, but I suddenly wanted to run after you. There were things I desperately wanted to ask you. How were you living now? How have you spent the ten years since we parted? If Kiyotaka hadn't been with me, I might well have run after you.

Adjusting my pace to that of Kiyotaka, I began to walk ever so slowly toward Dokko Pond. Frayed, withering cosmos petals were swaying in the cool breeze. A distance that ordinary children could walk in ten minutes ended up taking a half-hour for Kiyotaka. Yet compared to before, he manages to get around, and

7

it has only been about two years now that he's been able to act on his desires. Recently, his teacher at the school for handicapped children has been saying that, with training and effort, he might someday be able to lead an ordinary life and hold a job.

We walked along the sun-dappled path beside the pond and boarded the lift to the top of the mountain. I scanned the slopes looking for you, but you were nowhere to be found. We descended a short distance from the summit through a grove of oaks to a large rock jutting out of the side of the mountain. I had Kiyotaka sit there, and for a long time we gazed at the scenery. There wasn't a cloud in the sky, and at about eye level a hawk circled endlessly. Way off in the distance, violet mist enveloped rows of mountains that bordered the Sea of Japan. I explained to Kiyotaka that it was the Asahi Range, and that the mountain rising up on the right was Mount Chôkai. I kept glancing all the while at a square gondola descending another of Zaô's slopes, thinking that you just might be inside. Every time I heard footsteps on the path behind me, I cautiously turned and looked, wondering if it could be you. Kiyotaka laughed as he watched the hawk and the gondola, which had become a tiny speck, and also when he spotted a column of smoke rising from somewhere below. I joined in his glee, all the time envisaging your features as they had looked to me for the first time in ten years. I kept thinking how much you had changed, and wondering why you had come to Zaô.

After sitting on the rock for what must have been nearly two hours, we decided to return to the inn. We took the lift down to Dokko Pond and back to the gondola landing stage. This time there were only the two of us on board, and once again I gazed at the autumn leaves, which were at their peak intensity. The whole mountain wasn't covered with crimson foliage—patches of bright red flowed past on both sides of the gondola, interspersed with evergreens, trees with brown leaves, and ginkgo-like trees with golden leaves. These other colors made the red leaves stand out even more, as though they were ablaze. Musing on their similarity to great flames spouting ever so gently from small openings in the inexhaustible array of hues, I gazed silently and intently at the coloration of the dense trees. Suddenly, it seemed as if I were looking at something frightening. A lot of different thoughts were racing through my head. Perhaps this sounds exaggerated, but what would no doubt take hours to express in words flashed through my mind each time a patch of leaves crossed my line of vision. You will probably laugh at my usual dreaminess, but I was intoxicated with the intense blaze of autumn leaves and definitely felt something threatening in it, rather like the quiet, cool blade of a knife. Perhaps our unexpected meeting reawakened my girlish tendency to fantasize.

That night, after Kiyotaka and I bathed in the inn's huge stone bath filled with steaming, sulfurous water, we again walked up to the dahlia garden to see the stars. Taking a shortcut the inn's employees had told us about, we followed a deserted, winding path, shining a flashlight to show us the way. It was the first time in his whole life that Kiyotaka had walked so much. The crutches were hurting his armpits, and he stopped several times in the dark to complain, but when I sternly urged him on, he changed his mind and proceeded little by little toward the illuminated circle cast by the flashlight.

We were out of breath by the time we reached the dahlia garden. Coming to a stop, we looked up at the night sky. Stars so great in number as to leave us awestruck were twinkling, seeming so close that we could stretch out our hands and touch them. The dahlia garden, which was on a gentle slope, was nothing but a faint scent and a dim outline, the colorful blossoms blotted out by the darkness. The only sound was of the wind. The mountains towering before us, the gondola-platform building, the pylons supporting the wires—all were engulfed in silent darkness, above which spread the shimmering Milky Way.

We reached the center of the garden and, keeping our eyes upturned to the heavens, walked farther and farther up the slope. At the top of the dahlia garden were two small benches. There we sat, dressed in the warm parkas we had purchased near Yamagata Station, transfixed by the glittering universe above us despite the discomfort of the chilly wind. Ah, what loneliness in all those stars! And what extraordinary fear that boundless expanse inspired in me! Somehow I couldn't help feeling that, after ten years, suddenly bumping into you in the mountains of this northeastern region was a sorrowful event. Why on earth should it have been sorrowful? As I gazed at the stars, I whispered in my heart: sorrow, sorrow. As my sorrow increased, the incident of ten years before came alive again, as if projected on a screen.

This may turn into a long, tedious letter which you might tear up before reading to the end. Even so, I intend to finish it. Or at least I want to set down plainly what I was thinking—and what led me to the conclusions I came to—at the time of the incident, which caused more pain to me than to anyone else (although you will perhaps lay claim to this distinction). I really ought to have talked about these things when I left you ten years ago, but I didn't. Now they all lie in the distant past, but I'll recount them again in writing.

It was five in the morning the day when I received the phone call. I was awakened in my upstairs bedroom by our maid, Ikuko, who said, "Your husband seems to be in real trouble." Her voice was shaking, and I could sense that it was something serious. I pulled a cardigan over my pajamas and raced downstairs. A deep, calm voice on the other end of the line said, "This is the police. What is your relationship to Arima Yasuaki?"

"I'm his wife," I answered, struggling to keep my voice from shaking from both the cold and my agitation. After a moment's silence I was told in a businesslike tone that a man who appeared to be my husband had attempted a double suicide in a room at an inn in Arashiyama. The woman had died, but he might be saved. He was receiving treatment at a hospital but was in critical condition. They wanted me to come right away. He gave me the address of the hospital.

"Last night my husband was supposed to be staying at an inn near Yasaka Shrine in Kyoto," I said. He asked me the name of the inn and what my husband was wearing when he left the house. I told him as much as I could remember, describing the color and make of your jacket, and the pattern of your tie. He told

11

me that it indeed seemed to be Arima Yasuaki and asked me to come to the hospital at once. With that, the man hung up.

At a loss as to what to do, I ran in a panic to Father's bedroom in the annex. He was just getting up. When I told him what I'd heard, he asked, "Are you sure it wasn't just a crank call?" But it hardly seemed possible that anyone would go to the trouble of making a crank call so early in the morning in the dead of winter. While Ikuko was calling for a cab, the doorbell rang. A voice on the intercom identified the caller as a policeman from the local precinct. They had been contacted by the Kyoto police station requesting confirmation that the message had been understood. It was evidently no prank. I clung to Father and begged him to go with me.

"Did they really say it was a double suicide?"

"They said the woman with him died."

We kept repeating these words as we got into the cab and sped along the Meishin Expressway toward Kyoto. It couldn't just be an accident; yet attempting a double suicide with a woman I didn't know didn't seem possible to me. Could I believe you would actually do that with another woman? Only two years had passed since you and I were married, and we had been going out together for a long time before we were engaged. We were even beginning to think of starting a family. I thought it surely must be a case of mistaken identity. You would have entertained your Kyoto clients at a nightclub in the Gion district, and when it got late you would have stayed at your usual inn by Yasaka Shrine.

However, when I arrived at the hospital in Arashiyama and

saw the man who had just been moved from the operating room to a bed in one of the wards, I recognized you immediately. There is no way I can put into words my shock and astonishment. I was so stupefied that I wasn't even able to go to your side as you lay receiving transfusions, on the verge of death. The policeman who had been waiting for us explained in the corridor outside the ward that the deep wounds had been inflicted by a fruit knife that pierced your neck and chest, missing the carotid artery by a hair's-breadth. Some time had passed before you were discovered, and you had lost a lot of blood. One of your lungs had been punctured, and by the time you were brought to the hospital, you had almost no blood pressure and your breathing was sporadic. The policeman said that the next few hours would be critical.

Soon a doctor appeared and gave us more details, saying your condition was still very serious and that he couldn't be sure whether you would live or not. The woman's name was Seo Yukako, a twenty-seven-year-old hostess from Club Arles in the Gion. The side of her neck had likewise been slashed with a fruit knife, and she had died almost instantly. The police asked me a lot of questions, but I don't remember how I responded. It was impossible for me to answer questions about you and Seo Yukako.

Father called his secretary, Okabe, and said somberly, "Something terrible has happened. Come to Arashiyama in my car immediately." He gave the address of the hospital and hung up, then looked at me, an unlit cigarette in his mouth, before turning his gaze to the scenery outside. For some reason I can vividly recall Father's face at that moment, and the dawn sky through the windows of the hospital corridor. He had the same expression as when Mother died, when, with an absentminded movement, he suddenly placed a cigarette between his lips. I was seventeen then.

The moment the doctor announced that Mother was nearing the end, I looked intently at Father as he sat by her bed. Normally unflinching, and never once having shown any sign of weakness, Father vacantly took a cigarette out of his breast pocket and put it in his mouth. When I think about it, that action was unexpected and out of place. Now, as he stood in the long hospital corridor, looking vacuously at the early morning winter sky which was beginning to take on a bluish cast, Father's expression and mannerism were the same as at Mother's deathbed. I experienced an ominous presentiment. I found some matches in my purse and lit his cigarette with fitfully trembling hands, as if numbed by the cold. Father glanced at my shaking hands and said laconically, "You don't care if he dies, do you?"

But I even lacked the composure to think of an answer to that. What on earth had happened? It would be different if it had been a sudden accident, but why had my husband attempted suicide with a nightclub hostess?

Until you regained consciousness two days later, your condition became critical twice. Yet you recovered, showing such a tenacious will to live, even the doctors were amazed. It should be called a miracle. Finally, I was able to hear from your own mouth what had transpired. Though it was a "double suicide," it was forced upon you. Seo Yukako, who had been planning to commit suicide, stabbed you in the neck and chest while you were asleep and then

slit her own throat. You had no idea why she did this, and made it obvious that you had nothing more to add. Even during the police interrogation at the hospital, you just kept saying you didn't know. At first, the police raised the possibility that it had been you who had forced the suicide, but when the circumstances and the nature of the wounds were considered, you were cleared of suspicion. Thus, you didn't plan a love suicide with Seo Yukako, but were an unfortunate victim who had become unexpectedly involved. You were lucky not to have died. The incident was over and done with, but it was I who remained unappeased. It ended up being reported in the newspaper as a love suicide involving the married section chief of a certain construction company. Your adulterous fling turned into a big, bloody scandal. To Father, too, who had thought of you as his successor, it was a huge shock.

Do you remember when the doctor said you could be released from the hospital after ten days? It was a warm, clear day. I had gone to the hospital with a change of clothes for you and a box of muscat grapes I had picked up on the way at a department store in Kawaramachi. As had become my habit since the incident, I walked down the long corridor from the waiting room to your ward feeling fearful and nervous. I had resolved not to ask a single question about what had happened until you had completely regained your strength, but each time I walked down the corridor an irrepressible wave of wretchedness and anger would well up inside me, and I was tempted to let you feel the full brunt of my fury, jealousy, and anguish.

When I entered your room, you were standing in your pajamas, looking intently out the window at the scenery. You saw me but didn't say a word, and just turned your gaze back to the scenery. I was wondering how, exactly, you intended to explain everything to me, your wife. Your wounds were almost healed, and it seemed the time was right for an accounting. The weather was fine, the heating in the room was rather high, and it seemed like a good day for discussing things calmly. And so, as I was putting your change of clothes away in the box beneath your bed, I opened my mouth, intending to say nonchalantly, "Well, let me hear an explanation." But what came out instead was entirely different; it was sharp and pulled no punches.

"This affair of yours has turned out to be pretty expensive, hasn't it?"

The floodgates opened. I was young, and could have hardly been expected to react any differently.

"You almost died. It's nothing short of a miracle that you survived." You remained silent, your back to me. Recalling the scene now, it seems I kept hurling abuse at your back: the incident was splashed across the pages of newspapers; every day it dominated the conversations of employees at Father's company, and you had become a laughingstock; even Ikuko had to hang her head when she walked through the Kôroen neighborhood. I steadily lost all composure and ended up screaming at you through my sobs. Your silence only infuriated me more.

"I'm not sure I can live with you any longer." Having let this out, I caught myself and fell silent; I sensed you and I might really end up separating. No matter how upset I had been since the inci-

dent, such thoughts never once had crossed my mind. I had felt nothing but hope that you would be spared, and wanted you not to die. I wasn't calm enough to think of anything else.

As I looked at your back, somewhere deep inside me grew cold, and I wondered why, exactly, we needed to part. Why had things come to this? Why did something unforeseen like this occur? Why was a happy couple like us driven into a situation where we had to separate? You maintained your silence, not venturing a single word.

Your attitude fanned the flames of my dissatisfaction. "So you don't intend to say anything?" The afternoon sunlight of early spring fell on the livid skin of your wound, and your face was like a Noh mask highlighted by a torch. Smiling faintly, you finally turned to me and spoke. And how shameless and arrogant were your words! You ought to have been able to say something else, and even now anger wells up in me as I recall them: "Are you saying, then, that if I apologize you'll forgive me?"

Oh, how awkward we were with each other. After relaying what the doctor said about discharging you in ten days, I left your room without having sat down. As I walked through the entrance hall of the hospital and out onto the asphalt path leading to the gate, I saw Father's car arrive. He poked his head out of the window and looked at me with a perplexed expression on his face, betraying the discomfiture he felt at running into me unexpectedly when he had come to visit in secret. There was evidently something he wanted to talk to you about, but perhaps he changed his mind when he saw me, and he urged me to get in the car. After

17

telling Kosakai, the driver, to stop when he found a coffee shop, he sank back into his seat, looking ever so tired. He kept flicking the lid of his lighter open and shut.

"To use a horse-racing term, the front legs have snapped in two. That's what this situation is," Father said in the small coffee shop we ended up in. With a grim expression, he added another analogy: "a jar shattered to bits." It didn't occur to me initially that he wasn't talking about our relationship as husband and wife but about your position in the company. When I realized what he meant, I understood just how grave the situation was. Father, a true entrepreneur, thought of you more in terms of his successor than as my husband. I'm sure you knew just how high his expectations of you were, since he had no heir. In a very autocratic manner, he had lined things up so you would succeed him at Hoshijima Construction. Of course, there were movements within the company to thwart his plan. Vice President Koike and his allies, Mr. Moriuchi and Mr. Tazaki, were not pleased when you joined the company. At the time, Father figured that he could remain on the job another fifteen years, by which time his son-in-law would be forty-two. This was how he was looking at things. Hoshijima Construction had been built up during his lifetime, but as it grew and developed, he gradually lost his single-handed control over it. Having made his younger brother senior executive director, a cousin executive managing director, and a nephew general sales manager, he had succeeded in keeping things well within the family, but you were no doubt aware that the situation began to change when he backed the shrewd Koike Shigezô as vice president. You were, so to speak, Father's ray of hope.

If you only knew what care he had put into choosing you as the husband for his sole daughter, you would surely be surprised. Only some time after we parted I heard about it. To begin with, Father had to deal with the fact that I wanted to marry a young man, Arima Yasuaki. You and I had been seeing each other since college, and we both wanted to get married. But Father wasn't willing to give his blessing for this reason alone. He enlisted the services of a detective agency and had you thoroughly investigated. And he didn't stop there. He had two other agencies check you out as well. Having lost your parents at an early age, you had been raised by an uncle, which appears to have been the cause of the greatest concern to Father.

I have never asked Father what the results of the three investigations were, but no particular problems appeared. When he met you in person, you were undoubtedly thoroughly scrutinized by his perceptive eyes. I heard his opinion of you from someone else: "Arima Yasuaki has something that endears him to people. As a person, that is certainly to his credit. But, as a businessman, I'm still not certain whether or not it's a disposition of the first order. Since I'm selecting him not as my daughter's husband but as my successor at Hoshijima Construction, I can't decide rashly." And I heard he talked quite candidly to an acquaintance about how difficult it was for him to reach a decision. This was highly unusual for Father, who always proceeded in a decisive, dictatorial manner. In other words, you might say he gave his blessing to our marriage because he had resolved that, after his death, Hoshijima

Construction would be entrusted to a young man named Arima Yasuaki, who was not a blood relation.

While we were sitting in the coffee shop, Father was smoking a cigarette and said, "It's no big thing for a man to have an affair or two. But something like this..." Then, heaving a deep sigh and fixing his gaze on me, he muttered the same words about the forelegs of the horse being broken and the jar being shattered as if he were saying the two of us would never be able to return to the way we were.

The same night, a man we had never met paid a visit to Kôroen. Father had left on the evening Shinkansen bullet train for a business trip to Tokyo, and only Ikuko and I were at home. When I talked to the man through the intercom, he identified himself as the father of Seo Yukako. Ikuko and I looked at each other, wondering whether we should see him or not. I was hesitant to let an unknown man into the house when only women were present, especially at night. But even more than this, I was apprehensive about what business the father of the late Seo Yukako could possibly have with me.

When we showed him into the parlor, the old man (he probably wasn't of an age one would call "old," but his small stature and grizzled hair made him seem elderly) bowed repeatedly and in a deferential manner. With a pained expression on his wrinkled face, he said that he didn't know how to begin apologizing for what had happened, and hung his head. I was at a loss for a reply, but said something about what a terrible shock it must have been to lose his daughter. I was worried that perhaps he wanted to pick a quarrel or something over what had happened, but the openness of his expression and manner put me at ease. As Seo Yukako's father—that is, as the father of the young woman who had caused the incident—he seemed unable to ignore the scandal and wanted to offer at least a word of apology before returning to Maizuru. It happened to be the forty-ninth day after Yukako's death, and he was on his way home after a simple memorial service in Kyoto.

He sat on the sofa for a while and, blinking his tiny eyes, said, "I would never have believed that my daughter and Mr. Arima had developed such a relationship." There was something strange about the way he said this, and I asked, "Did you know my husband before?" The old man then related something that stunned me: you and Yukako had been classmates in junior high school. He seemed to have recalled this only recently, for during police questioning he had completely failed to mention it. You were classmates only for a short while, when you went to live with relatives in Maizuru after losing first your mother and then your father. After just four months or so in Maizura you were taken in by your uncle and went to live in Ikuno Ward in Osaka. During those four months you got to know Yukako, who was in your class. You once went to visit her family, who ran a tobacco shop, and the old man said that even after you moved to Osaka you exchanged occasional letters with his daughter. When Yukako graduated from the local high school, she got a job at a department store in Kyoto. "I thought she was working at the department store all this time. I've no idea why she wanted to die. She didn't leave a note or anything." He bowed so low that his head almost touched the parlor floor, and said over and over, "Your home life has been disrupted, and your husband almost died. As a parent, I can't begin to apologize enough."

He departed, all hunched over and leaving the tea I had poured for him untouched. I sat absentmindedly in the living room for a long time, overcome by an indescribable sadness. I suddenly thought of the relationship between you and Yukako in terms of "love," and for some reason this loaded and palpable word planted itself in me. It occurred to me that what had existed between you and Yukako was not simply something physical between a man and a woman but a strong love that I could ultimately never penetrate. This thought gradually rose within me and began to fix itself as a conviction. If what I had dismissed as a simple dalliance between casual acquaintances was actually a secret and passionate love affair beyond the reach of anyone else...

I felt an insuppressible jealousy well up in me. Two images drifted hazily into my mind: a racehorse with its front legs broken and a jar smashed to pieces. As I sat in the living room, my head drooping, I recognized the truth of what Father had said: this incident was definitely an irremediable tragedy. You and I needed to discuss it calmly. The word "divorce" occurred to me. I felt as if the love I had for you was quietly melting away, to be replaced by a feeling of hatred.

I thought of the five years we had been lovers between meeting as college freshmen and our marriage when I was twenty-three, and of the two years and three months we had spent as a married couple. Then I pondered the fact that the connection between you and Seo Yukako had been even longer. Why didn't you tell me—or the police, for that matter—you had known her since junior high? Wasn't it because there was something you wanted to hide? Then I had a stroke of feminine intuition, and Yukako, a woman who was already dead and whom I had never met, was standing right in front of me. And you were beside her, your face turned toward me with the vacant, cold expression that you have when something is on your mind. Between you and Yukako there was a secret passion, a tragic and deep love to which my existence was irrelevant. Such a fantasy was typical of me. Perhaps you will not be able to stop laughing at what I have written, yet I believe in intuition on such occasions. The image of you with Seo Yukako, man and lover, has never disappeared from my mind.

The day before you were to be released from the hospital, to my surprise, it was you who suggested divorce. "I can't go back, either to the house in Kôroen or to Hoshijima Construction. I'm not that shameless." You laughed, dipped your head before me and, for the first time, apologized. It was curt, the kind of apology one could only expect from you, but I could see your mind was made up, and you were relieved.

I could barely stop myself from saying, "Seo Yukako's father recently stopped by the house at Kôroen. You and she had been seeing each other for a long time, hadn't you?" Instead, I said, "I should really get compensation for all this, don't you think?" And then, just to see your reaction, I asked, "I suppose you met her at a nightclub in the Gion, didn't you?"

You gave a slight nod and, looking out the window from

your bed, answered, "I was drunk, and I don't remember what led to it. You never know what will happen in this life."

Then we went out into the hospital garden and walked in the warm sunlight. I marveled at my composure, feeling as if I were gazing at flowing water with a calm mind. Oh, and to think that I had been so happy! Until the incident my life had been peaceful and fulfilled. What had happened? Lost in thought, I wondered if I might be dreaming. I also wondered if, in talking about divorce, you were pretending you knew nothing. Since you evaded me with, "I was drunk," I decided to feign ignorance also. Those were the things on my mind as we walked together among the bare poplar trees, you in your hospital gown.

Even now, I sometimes wonder why I didn't ask questions about what really happened between you and the woman who died. I didn't really understand my own feelings then, but now I feel I am able to analyze myself a bit more clearly. To put it simply, even faced with divorce, I was resting too comfortably on the happiness of the time we had spent together, first as lovers and then as newlyweds. Beneath this state of mind, there was a certain sympathy for you, wrapped in a hatred many times stronger. All of these things must have built up my self-esteem, making me reticent and impassive. It seemed as if I wanted to believe your relationship with Yukako was a casual sexual liaison. In other words, I didn't want to be humiliated by a dead woman I didn't even know.

The sunlight that day was a palpable sign of approaching spring. You said tersely that after your release from the hospital,

24

you would go and live with an uncle. Then you became silent. You spun your arms around, stopped, took deep breaths, did knee bends, and looked as if you felt quite refreshed. I kept recalling the slight, hunched-over, retreating figure of Seo Yukako's father.

After parting in the hospital garden, I took the train to Katsura and caught an express for Umeda. At Umeda, I went to the Hanshin Railway Station, intending to go back to Kôroen, but on a sudden impulse I walked down Midôsuji Boulevard to Father's office at Yodoyabashi. Sitting on the sofa in his office, I told him you wanted a divorce. He just said, "Is that so?" Then he took some money out of his wallet and placed it in front of me. "Here's some spending money. Do what you like with it," he said with a smile. I was sobbing like a baby as I thrust the wad of bills into my purse.

It was the only time I cried over our divorce, and I kept crying until my tears dried up. It wasn't so much about being sad; rather, I had a premonition of some forthcoming misfortune, and I was overpowered by an intense fear. The misfortune was threatening not just me but you as well, and I was trembling. I retraced my steps along Midôsuji Boulevard, surrounded by a crowd of office workers heading home in the gathering dusk. As I walked, with my head bent to hide my tear-stained face, I resolved to go through with the divorce. I felt as if I had been forced to board a ship against my will, and it was slowly pulling away from the dock. A month later, I signed the divorce papers you sent and fixed my seal on them.

I feel as if there are other things I wanted to write about, as if this isn't what I intended to write. And now a thick letter piles up before me. It must be the loneliness I felt as I looked at the stars from the dahlia garden on Zaô that made me want to take up the pen. This letter is also the result of the lingering feelings I had on seeing your lonely profile after ten years. You looked so forlorn when I saw you in the gondola going up Mount Zaô, even more than when you were lying on the hospital bed with a serious wound. Your eyes projected a powerful manifestation of darkness, fatigue, and despair. It troubled me greatly, and after several uneasy days I hit on the silly idea of writing to you.

Although there is no longer anything between us, I don't want to think that divorce has brought us mutual unhappiness. If it has, then what I felt in Father's office on the day we parted was not merely an ominous presentiment. Because I parted from you, I had Kiyotaka. I can hardly describe the distress and pain I felt when I became aware of Kiyotaka's infirmity. I saw this child of mine, who wouldn't try to sit up even though he was over a year old, and it occurred to me that my premonition had been fully realized. I even thought it was you who had brought the fate of having a handicapped child upon me. If it hadn't been for the incident, we wouldn't have divorced. And I would have had your child, and we would have lived happily and in peace. It was all your fault. I remarried, to a man recommended by Father, an assistant professor at a university, and had Kiyotaka. And wasn't it because we separated and I married Katsunuma Sôichirô that I had a child like Kiyotaka? I was often lost in such thoughts. I despised you.

Perhaps you will say that I was unfairly taking it out on you. True, but at that time I was quite serious about connecting the birth of Kiyotaka to your infidelity and the bloody affair that went with it.

However, after the initial shock and grief of having a disabled child subsided—to be replaced gradually by a new maternal affection and resolve—my hatred of you vanished. Your image grew fainter in my mind. During the four years between Kiyotaka's third and seventh birthdays, I carried him back and forth to the Hanshin Physical Therapy Center. Each day was a struggle, but on the day he was finally able to stand, I wept, and wept again when he walked with the support of a railing. But his handicap was comparatively light. Eventually he was able to speak, although with difficulty. Then he managed to walk with crutches and attend an elementary school for handicapped children. Now that I can see a ray of hope in his future, I have come to feel I'm leading a fairly happy life, though of course it's not without its dissatisfactions. I was determined not to let our divorce make me unhappy, and that resolve has remained with me like an obsession. I certainly didn't want you to be unhappy, either, and this thought, too, has persisted.

With that, I shall conclude this long letter. While writing on and on at such length, I have become unsure what it's for. I have an urge to tear it up, but I'll mail it with just one purpose: to let you know about the visit by Seo Yukako's father. I'm not sending it with any expectation of a reply. Please take it as an explanation—ten years late in coming—of our parting, with all its equiv-

27

ocation and lack of clear intent. Please take care of yourself in this cold weather.

> Sincerely,
> Katsunuma Aki

P.S. So that you would immediately recognize the sender, I put my maiden name, Hoshijima Aki, on the envelope. I got your address from Mr. Takiguchi in the Materials Division. I had heard he was on close terms with you until recently.

March 6

Dear Aki,

I read your letter, and immediately afterwards I didn't feel in the least like replying. But as the days passed I realized that I, too, had a lot of issues I never talked about. So I am now writing back, though not without some reservations.

You wrote about our separation as being somehow ambiguous and not clearly intended, but you are mistaken. As far as I was concerned, there was a definite reason why we needed to part: the disgraceful incident of which I was the cause. Though I was a married man, I had an affair with another woman that escalated to a scandalous event; there was no way I could justify what I had done. I don't think there could have been a more compelling reason for a divorce. I upset too many people. I suffered an injury, but the wound inflicted on you was undoubtedly much greater. I also wounded your father and Hoshijima Construction. It was only natural that I should seek a divorce.

However, leaving all this aside, as a courtesy to you I would like to begin this letter by writing about my relationship with Seo Yukako. Let me apologize for having deceived you for so long. I'm sure you will understand the reasons for my not talking about it at the time of our divorce. It may sound pretentious of me to say so, but I didn't want to hurt you any more than I already had. And, besides, didn't you conceal from me the fact that you had met Yukako's father and that he had told you about me? If you had been candid with me, I might have given in and told you everything in the hospital garden. But you said nothing. You wrote about feminine intuition, but as I read your letter I had the impression it was a frightening perceptiveness that could penetrate to the core of anything.

I got to know Yukako in my second year of junior high school. Having lost both my parents, I was first taken in by my maternal relatives living in Maizuru. They were a childless couple named Ogata, who intended to eventually adopt me. I was at the difficult age of fourteen, and we were unable to arrive at an immediate decision about our compatibility, so I lived with them for a while until we could see how things would go. Thus, although my name was not entered in their family register, they provided for me and enrolled me in a local junior high school.

That was well over twenty years ago, and I barely remember what kind of youth I was or what I used to think about. But one thing I do recall clearly even now is my intense and utter loneliness—as if my heart were shrinking—when I first got off at East Maizuru Station. It seemed a strangely dark and dreary place, like an impoverished hinterland swept by chilly sea breezes.

East Maizuru was indeed a sleepy town on the northern border of the Kyoto region, facing the Sea of Japan. Snow in winter, humidity in summer, and the other seasons marked only by leaden skies and thick clouds, sparse traffic, and dust-laden winds from the sea. It's impossible to say how much I longed to return to Osaka,

30

but there was nowhere for me to go back to. Even the Ogatas soon seemed to regret having taken me in. We were always reserved with each other, and it was one awkward, constrained day after another. Both my uncle, an honest man who worked for the town's fire department, and my aunt, a quiet, modest woman who was born and raised in Maizuru, made every effort to be like parents to me; but since I would not open up to them at all, they were at a loss about what to do with me.

I wasn't able to make friends at school. I'm sure my classmates were also uncertain how to relate to a reticent city boy who had just lost his parents. Several months passed without my warming up to either school life or living with the Ogatas, but one thing did happen which made my heart beat faster: I was attracted to a girl in my class. There were many unsavory rumors about her: she was having a secret affair with a high school student; she already had carnal knowledge of men; a gang of delinquents had fought over her—gossip buzzed around her. During the brief period I lived in Maizuru, the only vivid thing I experienced was my love for this girl, Seo Yukako.

Shutting myself up in the six-mat room the Ogatas had given me, I wrote countless letters to her—letters I was determined never to send. When I finished writing one, I would put it in an envelope, hide it at the bottom of my desk drawer for two or three days, then burn it in the empty lot out back. Even now when I recall my feelings for Yukako, it wasn't just the faint, amorous longing of a pubescent boy; it was a single-minded passion of frantic intensity. Given the peculiar environment in which I found myself, perhaps the letters were a way of keeping my mind off the loneliness I felt. Yet I did nothing more than steal glances at her profile from a distance, and didn't speak to her or find any means to convey what I felt to her.

My feelings were genuine and strong, yet they were only those of a fourteen-year-old boy. Compared to other girls her age—the way she laughed, talked, walked, or crossed her legs—in every aspect she seemed sophisticated and mature. Perhaps it was the gloomy, lifeless atmosphere of a coastal town like Maizuru that amplified the rumors surrounding her into something awesome and mysterious. Every time I heard salacious tales about her, my feelings for her grew more intense. And she seemed eminently worthy of such scandals, reeking as they did of sinfulness. This is how beautiful and stylish she appeared in my eyes.

It was an early November day, with the type of piercing cold wind that blows only in Maizuru. (Perhaps you'll laugh, wondering what this conceited man will write next, but every time I think of Yukako taking her life at the inn in Arashiyama, I am also poignantly aware of what happened on this day more than twenty years ago.) After coming home from school, I went out again and walked toward the harbor. I don't remember why I set out or where I was going. On the jagged eastern side of Maizuru Bay was a desolate harbor known as Maizuru East Harbor, where several small fishing vessels were always docked. The grimy harbor wall zigzagged away into the distance, and the cries of sea birds mingled with the chugging of the boats' diesel engines. For some time I gazed at the harbor scene, leaning against the wall.

Each time I looked at the sea, it would fill me with a sense of sadness and longing to return to Osaka. Each time I looked at the sky, its grayness would make me yearn for my departed parents. Human beings are strange creatures and can sometimes vividly recall trivial things from the distant past, and I remember a woman with a towel tied around her head riding past me on a bicycle with a child sobbing on the back. The child's eyes met mine for an instant, and even now I can see, in perfect detail, those pupils swimming in tears.

As soon as the child's wailing was out of earshot, I noticed Yukako in her school uniform, facing the harbor and walking slowly in my direction with her hand on the top of the harbor wall. She was ambling along looking pensive and stopped only when she was about to bump into me. Startled, she glared at me as I stood there, and I completely lost my composure. Though we were in the same class, we had never spoken to each other before. She asked me what I was doing here. I managed to stammer out a reply of sorts. She appeared to consider something for a moment, then said she was about to board a boat and invited me along. When I asked her where we would go, she eyed a fishing boat moored nearby and said we would circle the bay once and come right back. She muttered to herself that if he knew she had someone with her, he might not take her, but she started walking toward the boat anyway.

I followed her, thinking she surely wouldn't want to board. I hesitated, sensing something bad would happen, but to just leave would be a lost opportunity, so I traipsed after her in the breeze blowing from the sea. A young man was standing on the boat named the *Ôsugi-maru*. When he saw Yukako, he smiled and waved, but his expression changed to a sharp look when he noticed me following. He had very short hair—almost a buzz cut—so at first I mistook him for a high school student, but depending on how you looked at him, he could just as well have been taken for a man of twenty-two or twenty-three.

Standing on the jetty, Yukako looked up at the man and introduced me as a classmate who had transferred from Osaka, adding that she had brought me along because I wanted a ride. The man looked me over with searching eyes and, with a slight nod, went into the cabin and started the engine. He then motioned for us to get on. Immediately after the boat pulled away from the jetty, the man asked me loudly if I could swim. When I said I could a little, he dashed out of the cabin, grabbed me by the collar, and threw me overboard. At the moment when I surfaced and looked toward the boat, I saw Yukako in her school uniform diving in after me. The man shouted something at us, but we swam desperately until we reached the jetty.

After I crawled onto the jetty and pulled Yukako out, we began running in our soggy clothes. We stopped a short distance away, afraid that the man might come after us, but the boat just continued on into the harbor and showed no sign of turning back. We had lost our shoes while we were swimming, and both of us stood there in wet socks, dripping seawater. I started walking away, but Yukako called me to stop. She caught up and grabbed my hand, apologizing again and again. Then she suddenly burst into high-pitched laughter. She laughed so hysterically that I just stared at her blankly. Drenched to the skin, she seemed convulsed with mirth as she held my hand. After this continued for some time, she invited me to her house. The sea around Maizuru is cold in November, and we were beginning to feel the chill. I began to have spasms of shivering, and she suggested that I change into her older brother's clothes. Under the scrutiny of passersby, we trotted from the harbor into town and hurried toward Yukako's home.

Her house was on the outskirts of town, some distance from my uncle's, on a street lined with factories that processed dried fish. These were just wooden buildings with black slate roofs, but a strong fishy odor pervaded the area, and packs of stray dogs loitered near the stacked-up wooden trays of fish. Yukako's house was a small, two-story building with a tobacconist's sign in front. Her mother, sitting near the window of the store, gasped when she saw us. Yukako explained that we fell into the sea when we were playing on the jetty, and asked her mother to fetch some of her brother's clothes. While Yukako changed upstairs, I got out of my wet clothes in the wood-floored changing room by the kitchen, dried myself, and put on clothes that reeked of mothballs which her mother had found for me. Yukako's brother had graduated from a local high school that year and was working at an automobile company in Osaka. I had heard there were only two children in the family, but I never met her brother.

After Yukako finished changing, she called to me and I went upstairs. She was wearing a red sweater and was drying her hair with a towel. Placing an electric heater in the middle of the room, she told me to warm up before I left so I wouldn't catch a cold. Her mother served us hot tea. Yukako and I sat with the heater between us for some time, sipping our tea in silence. On her desk were a reading light, a small wooden box, and a ceramic doll. Sometimes even now I recall the little-girlishness with which those items were arranged. The innocent, modest atmosphere of the six-mat room was entirely at odds with the gossip about her. Yukako, whose wet, glistening black hair was clinging to her shoulders and whose cheeks were warmed by the heater, exuded sensuality tinged with a certain darkness. To my eyes, everything about her evoked a mature woman who, fresh from bathing, dries her hair, lost in silent reverie.

But this isn't how I really saw her then. It would be more correct to say that this is how I picture the junior high school student Seo Yukako of over twenty years ago as I write this letter. I asked her, "Why did you jump in?" With a mischievous smile, she explained that she didn't want to be left alone with that man. I pressed her further, asking why, if she didn't want to be alone with him, had she intended to get on the boat with him. At first, she only glared at me with a defiant look in her eyes, but finally explained that he often waited for her to return from school, that he had been persistent in his invitations, and that if she didn't give in, she would never be rid of him. I mentioned the gossip I had heard about her and asked whether it was true or not. She said some things were true and some were not, and then asked me never to tell anyone what occurred that day.

The small heater had warmed my forehead, cheeks, and

palms. I finally stopped shivering, and a relaxed feeling surged over me. I succumbed to the illusion that Yukako and I had been close childhood friends, and I reproached her, saying in effect that the rumors must be her own fault, that she must unconsciously flirt with men. "That's not true," she said emphatically and, biting her bottom lip, glared at me for a long time.

Yukako's eyes had a certain sadness and emphasized her natural beauty. Looking at her, I was suddenly overcome by the oppressive, desolate feeling that often swept over me. The strange darkness emanating from Yukako had the same quality as the remote harbor town on the Sea of Japan. I told her how much I hated Maizuru and how much I wanted to go back to Osaka. It was getting late, and the room was growing dark. Only the glow of the heater's spiral element was visible. As I write about it, the scene emerges in my mind as if it happened yesterday. I have kept my memory of that time locked up in my heart as a phantasmagorical, dreamlike, ephemeral treasure. Even after reaching adulthood and marrying you, I often basked in that memory.

She stretched out her hands, placed them on my cheeks, and, with perfect composure, pressed her forehead against mine. Peering into my eyes, she giggled, unable to suppress her laughter. No matter how much I think about it, her behavior wasn't that of a fourteen-year-old girl. Recovering from my surprise, I gave myself up to whatever she wanted as if I were intoxicated. She whispered that she had liked me before, but that today she had really grown fond of me. She rubbed her cheek against mine and covered me with kisses. The ability of a fourteen-year-old girl to act toward a boy like that, without reservations, no doubt revealed Yukako's karma. I don't understand the deeper meanings of "karma," but whenever I think of her, this word has the most appropriate ring to it.

At the sound of footsteps on the stairs, we hurriedly let go of each other. It was Yukako's father, who had come home from work. He was employed at a fish processing factory and also ran a tobacco shop. Yukako introduced me, explaining about my having lost my parents and having come to Maizuru as my uncle's adopted son. The way she talked projected a young girl's presumption on her father's indulgence. Vanishing without a trace was the mature womanliness she had exuded as she rubbed her face against mine and whispered sweet words. After receiving my wet school uniform and underwear bundled up in a cloth, I took my leave. Yukako accompanied me as far as the front of the fish processing plant, then said goodbye as if nothing had happened. My association in Maizuru with Seo Yukako was limited to this one day.

When I returned to my uncle's house in those baggy clothes, holding the cloth bundle, I found my father's older brother, who lived in Osaka's Ikuno Ward, waiting for me. He had apparently reached an agreement with the Ogatas and had come to Maizuru to take me back with him. He told me that he had sent me to Maizuru at the Ogatas' urging, but, after all, taking care of me was his responsibility. Thinking of my future, it would probably be better for me to live in Osaka, he said. Though he was not well-off by any means, as long as I was willing, he intended to be a father to me until I grew up and became independent. Then he asked me to go back to Osaka. The matter had already been settled without waiting for my answer, and I was pleased to be able to return to Osaka, but I felt it would be unkind to the Ogatas to agree hastily, so I said that I wanted to give it some thought and went upstairs to my room. Here and there on my body the memory of Yukako still lingered from a short while ago, and with mixed feelings I leaned against the wall, lost in thought. Her saying today that she had really grown fond of me had severely shaken my resolve to return to Osaka. But although I was only fourteen years old, it was amply clear how the Ogatas felt about me. I decided there was nothing to do but go and live with my uncle in Osaka.

The same evening, my uncle and I called on my homeroom teacher at the junior high school and explained the situation, saying that although it was rather sudden, I would like to leave Maizuru the following day. The next morning I went to Yukako's house to return her brother's clothing and underwear that I had borrowed. She had just left for school. I explained the situation to her father briefly and, after getting their address, had to run back to where my uncle was waiting since the train was about to leave. So I left Maizuru for Osaka in a rush, without saying goodbye to Yukako or my classmates.

As soon as I was settled in my uncle's house in Osaka, I immediately wrote to Yukako. I've since forgotten what I said, but I soon got a response from her. I wrote to Yukako's Maizuru address once a month, and she answered two or three times, but then stopped. The next year I went on to high school. Every now and then I would recall her profile, feeling as if the memory would drive me mad, and I don't know how many times I thought of going to Maizuru to meet her. Yet, in spite of my ardor, before I knew it I had stopped writing to her, too. In the absence of any contact, Yukako began to seem quite remote, far out of my reach. I began to think her behavior toward me in her room was nothing more than a diversion to her, something never to be repeated. I plunged into studying for the university entrance exams and told myself that she had probably gone on to a high school in Maizuru, where she was no doubt the object of even more colorful gossip, and that she had long forgotten the likes of me. I tried to forget her, but then something would set off an image in my mind—Yukako with her wet hair clinging to her shoulders and her suppressed laughter in that upstairs room in the gathering dusk, or the meanings of those whispered words that seemed to palpitate along with my heart.

I got to know you during my third year at the university. As you often liked to cajole me into repeating, even after we were married, my heart was stolen by a certain coed sitting on the campus lawn eating ice cream amid a large group of classmates. You made me repeat this until it got tiresome. It is even more idiotic now, but let me repeat it once more: I truly fell in love with you at first sight. I devised every means I could to get your attention. It was as if every trace of Yukako had vanished from my heart, to be replaced by a vivacious, well-adjusted young lady. Yet Yukako was still lurking within me, as I became aware much later.

About a year after we were married and I joined Hoshijima Construction Company, a certain machine maker wanted to build a factory in Maizuru and requested that the construction be a joint project with a local company. In order to inspect the site, I set out for Maizuru accompanied by the chief of operations and the head of the planning department. It was the first time in more than ten years that I had visited Maizuru. We finished the work in no time and checked into an inn near the station, where we had an early dinner. Feeling nostalgic, I wanted to see the town and harbor and, setting out from the inn, I walked in the direction of the Ogatas' house. Mr. Ogata had passed away two years previously, and I thought Mrs. Ogata would be living by herself. Unfortunately, she was not at home. Having nothing else to do, I began walking toward the harbor, when I suddenly wondered how Yukako was doing. Perhaps she was already married with children. As if of their own accord, my feet turned in the direction of where her house had been.

Maizuru had completely changed, and the fish processing factories were now bigger, but the Seo family tobacco shop looked exactly the same. Yukako's mother, who appeared quite elderly, was sitting by the window. I bought some cigarettes, stealing glances inside the house, then resolved to address her. I identified myself, mentioning that I had been in the same class as her daughter in junior high school, that we both fell into the sea, and that she gave me a change of clothes. I asked how Yukako was doing. Her mother thought for a moment, then asked if I was the boy who went back to Osaka and occasionally wrote to her afterward. When I answered in the affirmative, she appeared to be stirred by fond memories and took the trouble to come outside, where she bowed deeply and told me that Yukako was now working in a department store in the Kawaramachi district of Kyoto. She said that her daughter was in the bedding section and asked me to stop by and see her if I had occasion to go to Kyoto. When I said that I had assumed she was probably already married with children, her mother laughed and said she never listened to her parents but lived as she pleased and was having a good time. Perhaps I knew an eligible man I could introduce her to?

I walked through the darkened streets of Maizuru toward the harbor, where I leaned against the harbor wall and looked out at the sparkling lights around the bay. It was there that it occurred to me for the first time that perhaps the memories of Yukako tucked away deep inside me were nothing more than the sort of sentimentalism about the past anyone feels. Ah, what fond memories! I had unexpectedly run into Yukako here, and was thrown into the sea by some guy I had never seen before. Back then, I had lost my parents, was taken in by the Ogatas, and moved to Maizuru, but inside I was full of loneliness and anxiety. What had I been thinking about to become infatuated with Yukako? Even so, what a peculiar girl she was! Such were my musings as I stood there for a long time, buffeted by the wind from the sea. Yukako's ghost suddenly departed from me. Without a doubt, I had been exorcised. I sensed it so vividly. My heart felt buoyant and, smoking one cigarette after another, I walked back to the inn in front of the station.

On a rainy day several weeks later, I was traveling in a company car to a hospital near Maruyama Park in Kyoto. I was going to visit the business manager of one of our client companies who had been admitted there. I had the driver stop near the Kawara-machi intersection and looked about for a fruit stall. Right in front of me was a department store, and I entered it intending to purchase a melon or something to take as a gift. As they were wrapping the melon, I suddenly remembered that Yukako worked in the bedding section of the same department store. My heart began to pound. (I know it was very self-indulgent for a man who had been married less than a year, but all I can say in my defense is that's how men are.) I went up to the bedding section on the sixth floor without any intention of speaking to her; rather, it was simply to see what kind of woman she had become. I loitered in the bedding department, stealing glances at the female salesclerks, but didn't see any who looked like Yukako. All of them had name tags on the front of their uniforms, but no Seo Yukako. Sometimes I wonder how things would have turned out if I had just left then, but I fell into one of those irresistible traps along life's path.

I asked one of the salesclerks whether there was someone named Seo Yukako, whereupon she opened a door to a back room and, before I could stop her, called, "Miss Seo, you have a customer." Yukako immediately came out and stood before me with a puzzled look on her face. By that point, things had gone too far for me to leave without saying anything.

I told her my name and studied her expression. Of course, she returned my look suspiciously. Speaking quickly, I repeated what I had said to her mother a few weeks previously, adding that since I happened to be in the store, I was stirred by old memories and wanted to say hello. She finally remembered who I was, and

at that instant a smile lit up her face—a smile with the same quality as the one so many years ago.

In her uniform, Yukako appeared more subdued than I had
pictured, but as her eyes and smile widened, the same beauty that
had occasioned so many colorful rumors reappeared. There was
no doubt that the person standing before me was Yukako. I was a
bit surprised that her face looked so pure, bearing no trace of the
vulgarity peculiar to women who reached adulthood after a somewhat wayward adolescence. She looked at me with eyes full of
nostalgia. It would be no problem for her to leave work for a half
hour or so, she said, and suggested that we go to a coffee shop
next to the department store, since it was rather odd to stand there
talking. But once we were seated across from each other in the
coffee shop, we had no idea what to talk about, and I just kept
rambling on about my memories of Maizuru. When I paused, she
said wistfully, "I'm going to quit the department store soon." She
added that she had been working part-time at a nightclub in the
Gion, and after giving the matter some thought she had decided
to make it her main line of work. From her uniform pocket she
pulled out a box of matches from the club and handed it to me.
When I mentioned that we were entertaining more and more clients
at clubs in the Gion, she smiled and said that we should definitely
drop by. Since the company car was waiting for me, we parted
after that brief meeting. A whole month passed before I first took
some important clients to Club Arles, where Yukako worked.

I began writing this letter with the intention of leaving nothing unsaid about my relationship with Seo Yukako; but if I write

any more, it will end up being longer than the letter you wrote, and I've already made it too long. As I've said before, I've been disgusted with the whole thing, wondering if any of it matters anymore. As for events leading up to the incident with Yukako, you may use your imagination, drawing on any of the trite "man meets woman" stories. Why did Yukako take her life? Why did she stab me with the knife? I think there is no need to explain all this to you in detail. Moreover, whether or not there was actually, as you wrote, "a secret, passionate love between Yukako and myself that no outsider could ever penetrate… ," I can only say the whole episode is like a hazy dream, a reality I cannot ascertain. It seems I was passionate when I was a youth in Maizuru, but my feelings when meeting Yukako more than ten years later were nothing more than a turbid, carnal lust. For the grief and pain I caused you—and for having betrayed you—I offer my sincere apology. I am wearied by so much writing, and shall end here with a wish that your home life may always be happy.

Respectfully,
Arima Yasuaki

March 20

Dear Yasuaki,

The ancient mimosa tree in the garden has again produced an abundance of tiny, yellow blossoms this year. I am fond of these powdery blossoms and went out into the garden with my shears to cut some suitable branches for a flower arrangement. The blossoms scatter in a puff at the merest touch, and even as I was gingerly carrying the branches I had cut, the blossoms continued to disintegrate, so I had to stop.

Every time I hold mimosa branches, I am momentarily overcome by an odd sensation of pain and sadness. I never expected that you would respond, and when I held the thick envelope containing your letter in my hand, my heart pounded and I was afraid to open it. After reading it, I had a strange feeling, exactly like what I felt upon seeing the mimosa blossoms scatter. I didn't anticipate such a romantic response. I was both saddened and pained, wondering if it had not actually been written by someone other than Arima Yasuaki. What on earth were you trying to convey in your letter? What could I possibly understand from it? You were pleased to play only the prelude, and when the main theme was about to start, you suddenly announced that you were tired of playing and slammed the lid of the piano shut. It was a long prelude, with a sweet, mocking melody.

I didn't write to you in the first place expecting a reply, but having received one, I find it gives me a feeling akin to indigestion. I want to know what went on between you and Yukako, right up to the end. Why did she put an end to her life? And why did she try to take you with her? Now I really want answers. And I have a right to know. I've never once given thought to such questions, but reading the romantic story of your first love made me want to press you for answers. And there are other things I want to know. Why did you go to Mount Zaô? And what are you doing for a living these days? I would really like to know. Or perhaps I wrote a letter to you initially because I wanted to know such things, but your unexpected reply had the effect of waking a sleeping child.

It has been ten years since we parted, and our lives are no longer each other's business. And yet there is no way I will find closure unless you give me a full account of your romance. Won't you please write to me about what led from your reunion with Yukako in the Kyoto department store to the inn at Arashiyama? Also, it may be irrelevant, but my husband plans to go to America for three months at the end of this month. He will be lecturing on Asian history at a university there.

Yours sincerely,
Katsunuma Aki

April 2

Dear Aki,

I received your letter. Your anger is justified. After posting the letter, even I felt a little disgusted at myself. I spent several days feeling unsettled by the embarrassment and stupidity of having written something so mawkish and unbecoming for a man of my age. Yet I do not feel like continuing this correspondence with you. To be perfectly candid, it is annoying to get letters from you. I have no obligation to write in detail of my affair with Yukako, and I have no desire to take on something so troublesome. With this, I would like to end our correspondence.

Sincerely,
Arima Yasuaki

June 10

Dear Yasuaki,

How are you these days, now that we're into the gloomy rainy season? Only two months have passed since I received your letter asking me not to write anymore, but here I am, incorrigibly taking up the pen again, though with some hesitation and uncertainty. This time I suppose you might really tear it up without reading it. You are no doubt completely fed up, wondering why I am so persistent.

To tell the truth, I myself don't understand why I want to write to you. I don't understand what exactly it is that I hope to gain. I don't understand, but my feelings are now at a very high pitch, prodded by the urge to let you know what is concealed within me. Possibly, by having written to you, I returned to the same state of mind as ten years ago, immediately after our divorce. Please just indulge the whims of a foolish woman! Although I am fully aware what a nuisance it is—and am resigned to the fact that you might not read it—I have decided to try writing another letter. After all, you were the only person who used to bear silently with my every complaint and caprice.

I once read somewhere that a woman's greatest vices are her querulousness and jealousy. Assuming this is part of a woman's real nature, there are times I instinctively want to spit out all the complaints and envy that have accumulated in my heart. Ever since the incident, all sorts of indescribable, depressing feelings have solidified within me, making me wonder if my personality has not changed as a result. I still have questions I'd like to throw at you, and it's fine if you reply with silence. Like talking to a wall—or to an empty cavern—perhaps it's better for me if you don't answer.

It was nearly a year after we separated that Father broached the subject of my marrying again. I was for the most part living a sequestered existence at the Kôroen house. I had even entrusted all the shopping at the nearby market to Ikuko and spent my days alone in the upstairs bedroom, sitting by the window facing the garden, pretending to read a long, foreign detective novel I had no intention of finishing; or I would listen to the records you had forgotten to take; or I'd lie face down on the bed, attentive to every tick of the clock.

You recall the small river running beside the road from the house to the Hanshin Line station. I think it was about two months after our divorce that the Tamagawa Bookstore there went out of business, and the premises turned into a coffee shop named Mozart. Ikuko heard that it was run by a couple in their sixties who played only Mozart as background music, and she rather persistently urged me to go for a walk and stop by for a cup of coffee. I did this on a day after the rainy season had ended and the sun was blazing. On the way, I ran into two or three neighborhood women I knew, but although they wanted to speak to me, I deflected them with a slight nod and continued down the road in the blinding sunlight.

I wanted to see you. The heat reflected from the road was

making my forehead and back perspire, and I recall feeling some-what giddy. It kept occurring to me that I wanted to see you. What did I care what people thought? What did it mean to me that you were a "jar shattered to bits"? I should have been a bigger person. I should have been able to forgive you. It happens all the time, doesn't it, that a husband's heart is stolen by another woman? I had made a mistake that couldn't be undone. As I walked along, I wanted you to come back no matter what. I resented Father for working behind the scenes to make us part. And I felt a loathing strong enough to make my blood boil for Seo Yukako, a woman I had never even met and who was no longer in this world.

The coffee shop was built in the style of the guesthouses one often sees at countryside resorts, where people go to escape the summer heat. Both the exterior and interior highlighted the natural beauty of tree bark, as if a mountain cottage had been removed and planted there. The beams in the ceiling were thick, exposed logs, and the chairs and tables were handcrafted, with the shapes of the knots and the grain of the wood suggesting careful selection. Though the café was small, it was constructed with the utmost fastidiousness and with no expense spared. Just as Ikuko had said, Mozart's music was being played, though a bit more loud-ly than one would expect. I was able to identify only one piece: the Jupiter Symphony. When the owner, wearing black-rimmed glasses with thick lenses, brought a glass of water to my table, I said, "I heard that you play only Mozart."

He laughed and asked, "Do you like music?"

"I do, but I don't know much about classical music."

"If you keep coming here for a year, you'll come to appreciate Mozart. And if you appreciate Mozart, you'll understand all music."

Holding a large silver tray against his chest, the owner spoke with a note of pride as he turned his ruddy-cheeked face toward the ceiling. He had a funny way of speaking, and when I giggled, he told me, "The record playing now is the Forty-first Symphony."

"That's the Jupiter, right?"

"Ah! So you do know, after all! You're right. It's the Jupiter. Symphony No. Forty-one in C Major, Mozart's last. It's a masterpiece with a fugue in the fourth and final movement that builds up to a vigorous finale, reiterating the sonata form of the first and second movements."

With that, he listened intently for a while, then whispered, "It's after this. The fourth movement is about to begin."

I ordered coffee and listened attentively to Mozart's majestic symphony, looking around the shop at the same time. Beside a framed reproduction of a portrait of Mozart was a small shelf with books about the composer. I was the only customer, and when the Jupiter ended I was suspended in a silence that seemed to absorb me. What a strange stillness it was! Again, I felt a strong desire to see you. Soon another piece of music began. The owner came by my table and, in the manner of a schoolteacher instructing a young pupil, said, "This is the Thirty-ninth Symphony, a veritable marvel composed of sixteenth notes. The next time you come by, I'll put on *Don Giovanni*. And after that the Symphony in G Minor. I think you'll gradually come to understand the human miracle that Mozart was."

The coffee tasted good, and the owner was quite congenial. Two or three days later I went again. There were many customers that day, and though the owner did his best to look after me as I sat by the window, he was very busy behind the counter, boiling water for coffee, making juice, and hurrying to put on a new record every time one ended. His wife, whom I had not seen the first time, was carrying orders to customers, keeping their glasses filled with water, and clearing tables. A piece I didn't recognize was playing. Holding my coffee cup to my mouth with both hands, I gazed vacantly at a young man who, with eyes closed and head bowed, was listening intently to the music. He looked very solemn as he concentrated on the quiet symphony. His posture and facial expression made it seem as if he were either offering a prayer to some great being, or as if he'd been scolded by someone who frightened him and was showing contrition with his entire body.

Until then, I had had almost no interest in classical music and had not thought that I possessed the sensibility or cultivation to understand the "human miracle that Mozart was." But as I studied the bearing of the young man and listened to the quiet symphony, a certain word sprang to mind: death. I have no idea why it occurred to me. Of course, I didn't wish to die at that moment; nor did I have an overwhelming fear of death. And yet the word *death* crystallized inside and wouldn't leave. As I sipped my coffee, I listened seriously to Mozart for the first time, with the word *death* tucked away somewhere in my mind. It was the first time in my life that I had ever listened to a piece of music with such serious, rapt attention. What had until then been merely an unexceptional symphony began to seem like an incomparable, exquisite melody, and at the same time like a mysterious refrain that hinted at a hopelessly evanescent world. How could a young man of around thirty have created such a beautiful melody two hundred years ago? How was he able, without using words, to convey the coexistence of sadness and joy, and do it so compellingly? Captive to such thoughts, I stared out the window at the newly leafing cherry trees that lined the street. Whimsically conjuring up the appearance and expression of Yukako—who was dead, whom I had never met, but who was no doubt far more beautiful than I—I surrendered myself to the undulating strains of Mozart's symphony.

When a different piece of music began, the young man I had been watching thanked the owner, paid his bill, and left. Almost simultaneously, like an ebbing tide, the customers that had filled the shop got up and left one after another until I was alone. Only then did the owner emerge from behind the counter and introduce his wife, a woman not elderly—probably about fifty-five or fifty-six—but with lovely silver hair tied back neatly and wearing the same kind of thick glasses as her husband. As if taking a break, the couple sat down next to me and conversed between themselves for a while. Then the wife asked me, "Do you live around here?" When I said that my house was a ten-minute walk down the street toward the beach, she thought hard, her round eyes casting about restlessly, and mentioned several names. Among them were some families in my neighborhood, but she didn't mention mine.

"We're the Hoshijimas, the house just before the tennis club."

"Oh yes, I know that house. It's the one with the big mimosa in the garden, isn't it?"

She said that she had never seen such a splendid specimen and asked if she might have a few branches when it bloomed. (If you are still reading this letter, you will no doubt find all this excruciatingly boring. But since I'm writing in flagrant disregard of your wish that we discontinue our correspondence, I will write what I please.)

I ordered another cup of coffee and told the owner, "I've come to understand a little what you meant the other day by 'the human miracle that Mozart was.' "

He stared at me in astonishment. Behind his glasses, the laughter had gone from his eyes, to be replaced by a glow of excitement. His boyish countenance faced me for such a long time that I became embarrassed and added, "I'm single. But I wasn't until two months ago."

Thinking perhaps that my husband had died, he asked, "Was it illness? Or an accident?"

I answered straight out, "No, we divorced." I anticipated a cross-examination (after all, when I looked at the round, darting eyes of his hardworking wife, she seemed like the nosy sort of woman one finds everywhere), but they just said in unison, "Oh, is that so?" Then, without touching on the subject again, they told me how they had come to open the coffee shop. In this way I learned about their life and background.

The owner had been conscripted in 1941, and in the winter of 1945—the year the war ended—he returned from Shanxi Province in China. He was born in 1921, so he would have been twenty-four or twenty-five at the end of the war, while I was still yet to be conceived. Three years later he got a job at a bank through someone's good offices, and for the next twenty-seven years, until he reached retirement age in the fall of 1975, he worked as a banker. He was director of the Toyonaka branch in his last two years before retirement. Then he got a part-time position at an affiliated credit union, but the work consisted mainly of settling accident claims and acting as a bill collector. Feeling that he wasn't suited for the job, he quit after a year or so. But for more than ten years the couple had thought of running a coffee shop after he retired, and they had already decided on the name Mozart as well as on the style of the building and the interior decor. And yet—the owner continued—because of the marriages of their three daughters, in quick succession, they were forced to dip into the savings set aside for the shop. Then they couldn't find a suitable lot or building for sale in the area they wanted, and thus ended up delaying the opening by three years.

"I first discovered Mozart when I was sixteen years old," he said.

Ever since, he had been a fanatical devotee of the composer, spending all his paltry allowance on records. Even after he was conscripted and was shouldering a rifle in China, he added nostalgically, Mozart's melodies ran through his head. He told himself that in his sunset years he would open a coffee shop named Mozart, where customers would listen exclusively to that composer's music. It was with this goal in mind that he worked at the bank. Whenever there was any unpleasantness or trouble at work, he would remind himself of this aim. Looking forward to his retirement package that would provide the major part of the funds for the shop, he persevered in work he found neither interesting nor enjoyable. He reported gleefully that when he heard a bookstore near Kôroen Station had gone out of business, he and his wife jumped at the opportunity.

"When we saw it the first time, we knew this was the place. Nowhere else could touch it for location and accessibility. We had finally found what we were looking for, and this was where we would build our coffee shop. We were so excited that we could scarcely contain ourselves." The owner laughed, and looked at me again for a long time.

His wife added, "For him, it was nothing but Mozart. He didn't drink or gamble, he wasn't into fishing, and he didn't know how to play go or shôgi. When he got home from work, he spent the rest of the day carefully wiping and fondling his hundreds of Mozart records. At first, I was put off and thought I had married a real oddball." Then, with a laugh, she added, "But eventually I, too, quite naturally became a Mozart fanatic."

With exchanges like this, our conversation continued for a long time. It suddenly occurred to me to ask about the young man who had left earlier. The owner explained that he was also a Mozart fan and had a large collection of records, but he wanted to hear a famous recording that was no longer available and would come every day and ask to listen to the same piece of music.

It was nearly time for me to start getting supper ready, so I placed the money for my two cups of coffee on the table and stood up. The owner also stood up and asked with a smile, "You said a while ago that you had begun to understand 'the human miracle that Mozart was.' Could you tell me what you mean?"

Having been exposed to Mozart only in the past couple of days, it didn't seem that I'd be able to put my thoughts into words. Besides, I couldn't very well express my tentative impressions to someone who had listened with rapt attention to Mozart's music countless times. Yet, pressed by the serious glint in the man's eyes, I ended up saying in spite of myself, "Perhaps living and dying are the same thing. That's the great mystery Mozart's gentle music seems to be expressing."

I had meant to say that "the human miracle that Mozart was" involves his ability to convey, without words, the coexistence of sadness and joy, to veil this in the tones of wondrous music, and to express it all so simply and so pleasingly to his listeners. Daunted by the owner's penetrating stare, I gave an answer that had never so much as crossed my mind. It is possible that the word *death*, which had suddenly popped into my mind a while earlier, had not entirely vanished, and that under its influence I blurted out something I had not actually thought of before.

"Oh really?" the owner mumbled, continuing to stare at me.

I hurried home in the lengthening shadows of the setting summer sun. Without understanding what I could have meant by the words I had uttered, the image of Yukako again appeared in my mind. What kind of woman was she? Why did she take her own life after making love with you? For some reason, I was dead tired when I reached home.

During the months from then until winter, I went to the coffee shop two or three times a week. I occasionally took the Hanshin Line to Sannomiya in Kobe, or in the opposite direction to Umeda, to shop at department stores, but whenever friends from college—such as Terumi or Aiko, whom you also knew well— invited me to a film preview or a concert, I always declined and would instead stay cooped up at home. Both Father and Ikuko let me do as I pleased, though they secretly worried about me. Yet in such a seemingly listless and empty life, at least one pleasure had surfaced: I, too, had become a Mozart fan. I purchased recordings recommended by the coffee shop owner and listened to them in my room until late at night. I also bought books on Mozart at a large bookstore in Osaka and read them avidly. I grew very close to the owners of the coffee shop, and they presented me with my own coffee cup to use whenever I went there. They were surprisingly attuned to my moods, and on days when I didn't feel like talking, they immediately picked up on this and left me alone; and on days when I preferred conversation to listening to records, one of them would chat with me and keep me company. Yet neither of them ever touched on the subject of my divorce.

I have rambled on, piecing together memories from the past and turning them into another long letter. I'm weary of writing, yet I haven't set down a single thing of importance. In my next letter, I'll be sure to include what I really want to say. You would no doubt like to tell me to stop. Nevertheless, be assured that I'm going to write again. Even if you tear my letters up and throw them away, I am going to write. But today I will end here.

According to the newspapers, the rainy season will be a long one this year. It has already been raining for five days. Weather like this puts Kiyotaka in a bad mood. He was nearly cured of wetting himself, but lately he's regressed and has "accidents" before he can make it to the toilet. This only happens when it rains for days on end. It's strange, but human beings definitely behave in accordance with the rhythms of nature. But such a trifling thing will leave Kiyotaka so crushed, he will go for days without speaking to anyone. I can't bear to see him like that. I used to be very fond of rainy days, but for this reason I have come to detest them. Please take care of yourself.

Yours sincerely,
Katsunuma Aki

July 16

Dear Yasuaki,

What downpours we have had during this year's rainy season! I commented to Ikuko, half out of irritation, that thanks to all the rain we wouldn't have the usual summer drought because the water level in Lake Biwa would remain high, and that was wonderful, wasn't it? She reminded me that rainwater doesn't collect in lakes but flows into rivers and then drains into the sea. So no matter how much precipitation we have, the dog days of summer will cause the water level of Lake Biwa to drop. They say that the end of the wet season will be here soon, but our house already feels damp inside, and mold is growing on the walls, on the tatami mats, in the hallway, and even on doorknobs. But enough of that. This will be a sequel to my previous letter.

I distinctly remember it was February 6, exactly six months after I began going to Mozart. Shortly after three o'clock in the morning, I was suddenly awoken by the persistent wailing of a siren. I knew at once it was a fire engine. And not just one or two but several fire engines, converging nearby from both east and west. I threw a dressing gown over my shoulders, opened the curtains, and looked out. Flames were shooting up beyond the rooftops. In one area of the neighborhood a red glow was expanding, and exploding sparks were clearly visible. With my hand clutched to my breast, I stood transfixed for some time, wondering if it could be the coffee shop that was burning. The leaping tongues of flame were certainly very close to it. The owners lived in a condominium behind the station, so they wouldn't be in any danger. All the same, I got dressed and went downstairs.

"It's a fire, isn't it?" Ikuko said as she came into the hallway in her nightgown and, ignoring the cold, opened the front door to look at the red-tinged sky.

"It might be the Mozart coffee shop," I said, slipping on my sandals and dashing outside. Ikuko ran after me carrying a thick coat: "You'd better come back right away. It's not safe at this time of night."

The night was unusually cold. Bundled up in the fur-lined coat, I trotted in the direction of the leaping flames. After I had passed through the residential area and crossed the small bridge over the river, I could see that Mozart was burning. In spite of the late hour, a crowd of onlookers surrounded the conflagration, and seven or eight fire engines were parked next to the river. The fire's fury had reached a peak by the time I arrived. Built entirely of wood, the coffee shop was enveloped in an enormous blaze, and nothing could be done to save it. Thick jets of water gushing from several hoses converged on the roof, only to be swallowed up and disappear. I noticed the owner, still in his pajamas, grasping the rope that had been strung up to keep onlookers away and staring at his burning shop. Elbowing my way through the crowd, I reached his side and likewise held on to the rope. It was unbearably hot facing the blaze, but I stood next to the owner anyway, with both hands on the rope. Before the popping and crackling of wood and occasional showers of sparks that rained down, we watched the coffee shop turn into ashes.

I'm not sure when the owner became aware of me, but keeping his eyes fixed on the flames, he turned his head toward me and said near my ear, "It's wood, so it burns really fast." I looked for his wife but couldn't see her anywhere. Inquiring after her, I realized that my voice was shaking, perhaps from fear that she might be in the shop.

"She went home a while ago. I guess she couldn't bear to watch. She said I might catch a cold dressed like this, and that she'd bring me something more to put on."

I was relieved to hear that, and asked, "You can rebuild the shop, can't you?"

He gave a slight nod. "We have fire insurance. But twenty-three hundred records have been destroyed."

Neither weeping nor laughing, with a strange expression on his face, he continued to gaze at the shop. By now the blaze had subsided somewhat. Ikuko had told me to come back right away, but I, too, kept my eyes on the shop and decided to stand next to the owner until the fire was completely out.

"Who would have thought that something like this...," I said.

Smiling faintly, he replied, "When I heard that the shop was on fire, I lost my head and began to tremble uncontrollably. But when I saw the size of the fire and realized that it was beyond saving, a strange sort of peace came over me, or perhaps I should call it detachment. Since no one was inside..." Indeed, "detachment" was just the word to describe his expression and tone.

The burned-out roof caved in with a thunderous crash, and the accompanying wave of sparks was so tremendous that, as one organism, the onlookers automatically stepped back. The owner grabbed my arm to pull me away, but I withstood the momentary surge of heat and sparks. Why did I do something so dangerous? As I watched the flames, which died down only to spring back with a roar before subsiding again, I was thinking of you. I had the impression that if I moved my body even an inch, the image of you that had emerged in my mind would vanish. So I stubbornly stood my ground.

We had been forced into a divorce, but even so I imagined that you must feel the way I did.... There must be times when, walking through a crowd somewhere, you suddenly remembered me.... You must still love me.... So ran my thoughts.

The instant your face appeared before me—accompanied by an irrepressible regret at our having parted—a sudden gush of sparks roared to life, as if to awaken me from my fantasy, and then disappeared. Feeling as if I had been slapped hard on the face, I looked at the burned remains of Mozart, now covered with thick smoke instead of flames.

The owner said to me in a quiet voice, "'Perhaps living and dying are the same thing. Such is the strange workings of the universe that echoes within Mozart's music.' You said so yourself, didn't you?"

I stared at him, wondering what he meant.

After thinking a moment, he added, "I thought I knew more

about Mozart than anyone. I doubt many people have listened to his music more than I have, and I was confident I understood him. Yet what you said had never occurred to me. Since then, I have been thinking about your words and now I understand. As you said, Mozart was definitely attempting to convey in his music what happens to human beings after they die."

Perhaps due to his growing animation, his face turned disturbingly tense, and his ordinarily gentle eyes took on a gleam of intensity behind the thick lenses. I couldn't help thinking that the words I had said were slightly different from what he had been repeating to himself. I'm sure there was nothing about "the workings of the universe." No doubt, as he continued to recall my casual comment, he must have inadvertently added words that were not mine.

I said, "I'm sure I didn't say anything about 'the workings of the universe.' "

He turned to me puzzled: "Yes, you did. I remember it distinctly. You said 'the strange workings of the universe.' "

I thought that the owner must have deceived himself about that part, but I decided to let it go. The fire was almost extinguished now, except for pockets of glowing embers that looked like burning charcoal. Firemen in silvery gear continued hose them down.

Then the owner said loudly, "No, that wasn't it. That wasn't it. You didn't say 'workings of the universe.' I just fancied you did. What you said was…" He stared at me, trying to recall the words, oblivious to the fine soot covering the lenses of his glasses.

"'The workings of life.' Yes, that's it. I remember now. I'm certain that you said 'the strange workings of life.'"

Somehow I didn't think that was right either, and I returned his gaze with my head tilted dubiously to one side. He laughed and, infected by his mirth, I laughed, too. He bowed to one of the onlookers standing behind him and asked if he might have a cigarette. It was someone I had often seen in the coffee shop. The man obligingly produced a cigarette from his breast pocket and, as he was lighting it, solicitously asked the owner whether or not he had fire insurance. The latter repeated what he had told me. The onlooker then said, "Well, records are sold at music shops. You only need to start collecting again." Looking indignant, the owner, addressing no one in particular, mumbled that one could not longer get hold of many of the recordings. With that, he ducked under the rope to talk to a fireman.

I slipped past the crowd and hurried home through the deserted streets, upset at having seen Mozart go down in flames. With my eyes fixed on the ground, I brooded, thinking, "It's started, hasn't it? The unhappiness has begun after all." All the things I thought about while sitting on the sofa in Father's office when I decided to leave you had begun to come true. You remember, don't you, that in my first letter I wrote about my premonition that parting from you would herald some misfortune? Because of an unforeseen incident, you left me, and before a year had passed my favorite coffee shop had burned down and twenty-three hundred records of music created by a genius had burned. What more could I expect to lose?

Once in my room, I took off the thick coat and sat on the edge of the bed. The clock said a little past four. Sleep seemed out of the question, so instead I listened to one of my favorite Mozart pieces again and again, with the volume turned as low as possible. It was the Thirty-ninth Symphony, a recording I had purchased at a large record shop in Umeda that Mozart's owner had told me about. It was the piece that he had called "a miracle composed of sixteenth notes."

"Perhaps living and dying are the same thing...." I wondered why Mozart's music had prompted me to say something so inane. And I recalled the owner's words as we stood in front of the charred ruins of his shop—words I had definitely not uttered, words he had arbitrarily fashioned out of that bizarre line of mine: "The strange workings of the universe... the strange workings of life." To a young person like myself, it wasn't such a remarkable expression. Yet as I felt the ripple-like melody of Mozart's Thirty-ninth Symphony lapping at every nook and corner in the stillness of the bedroom at that late hour, it began to seem as if those words illuminated the countless mysteries of life—like a stage magician's elaborate sleight of hand. What was it that the owner saw as he watched Mozart go up in flames?

I lay down on the bed and closed my eyes. Soon images of the conflagration, of the crackling wood, and of the owner had vanished from my mind, to be replaced by vague, wordless thoughts blending harmoniously with the Thirty-ninth Symphony: the cool shade on that summer day when we first met as students; the empty glow of the taillights on cars along Midôsuji Avenue, where we so often walked hand in hand; the dull shimmer of the sea near Kobe seen from the Hanshin Line train that I had ecstatically boarded, with no destination in mind, the day Father gave us permission to marry. As I indulged in such reveries, for one fleeting moment I felt I understood what was concealed in the words spoken by the owner a short while ago: "The workings of the universe… the workings of life." But that was just for an instant. In my mind, the phantom of Seo Yukako suddenly reappeared. A mute woman with features and a body far more beautiful than mine was standing inside me. And she was dead, no longer in this world.

The next morning I was eating a late breakfast when Father suggested that, since I was so friendly with the owner and his wife, a consolation gift would be appropriate. Ikuko added that, in such circumstances, money would be most welcome. Reasoning that they would probably be busy for two or three days settling their affairs, I visited them four days later at their condominium with the consolation gift.

They were pleased to see me and welcomed me into the living room, bowing repeatedly and thanking me for taking the trouble to go out to the fire on a cold night. I could not persuade the owner to accept the money, but I didn't yield and left it on the table, saying it was Father's orders and I couldn't take it back with me. After much hesitation he relented, at which point another visitor arrived. This man also appeared to have brought consolation money, and was arguing about this in the hall with the wife when the owner, saying that it was a perfect opportunity to introduce us, called him into the living room. The man was thirty-two or thirty-three, tall, with sharply defined features. The owner introduced him as "my nephew, the oldest son of my late brother." We exchanged greetings appropriate to a first meeting. He was Katsunuma Sôichirô, my present husband. But I'll write later about the events that led to our marriage.

After taking my leave, I killed time in the bookstore in front of the station, leafing through women's magazines and loitering in front of the paperback shelves, scanning the spines. I felt like having a good cup of coffee somewhere, but I couldn't bring myself to try a new shop so soon after the loss of Mozart. It must have been a Saturday. When a train pulled in, several high school girls got off, and it would only be on Saturday that they would be going home just after noon. In the life I was leading then, the month, date, and day of the week were utterly irrelevant, and I gave no more than an idle glance at their school uniforms. It also occurred to me that, since Father's company was also open only till noon on Saturday—and since he had no plans afterward—he might be home by evening. Knowing Father, I had a presentiment that I could expect him to start bombarding me steadily with his views on some subject, and that he would do so gently but with a look of finality in his eyes.

How accurate premonitions sometimes turn out! When I returned home, Father was lying on the living room couch watching television. When he saw me, he said he had something he wanted to talk about and, pointing to the sofa opposite, motioned for me to sit down. Sometimes I am secretly surprised and even proud of the accuracy of my intuitions, but then how is it that this perceptive wife failed to sense an entire year of her husband's infidelity? Now that I think about it, I'm amazed at what a slippery, talented actor you were.

Lying on the couch and looking at the television, Father suggested that it was time I thought about my future. "You need to forget all that should be forgotten. Let me think of a way for you to do this."

Before I could say that I had already forgotten all about it, he suggested that I go abroad. "In short, it's a matter of closure. Let's see, where would be good? Paris? Vienna? Greece? Or you could even go as far as Scandinavia. Enjoy a leisurely trip abroad by yourself and come back with your life like a blank sheet ready to write on."

With eyes downcast, tracing the patterns on the Persian carpet, I said that traveling by myself in a foreign country seemed lonely, and I had no wish to do it.

"When I look at you, I feel so sorry for you I can't bear it."

At this, I looked up and saw there were tears in his eyes. It was the first time I had ever seen him in tears. He said that he never imagined his daughter would experience such misfortune, and that he had been the one who had brought it all on me. "If I hadn't designated Arima as my successor in the company, you two might have been able to settle that incident by yourselves. This sort of thing happens often enough. As long as your feelings for each other were mutual, in time you might have been able to get back together again. But as president of Hoshijima Construction I had to insist that he leave the company. It seems that I decided

70

too rashly. I was convinced that if Arima quit the company, he must also leave the Hoshijima family. But lately I've come to think that that wasn't necessary. Even if he was no longer qualified to succeed me in the company, that's no reason for him to have to leave you, is it? I should have thought things through. I should have assigned Arima to another job, allowed you to live separately until your wounds healed, and then kept an eye on things so you could get back together once time had passed. That would have been the mature thing to do. I didn't actually tell Arima what he should do, but my way of putting it as a father left him no choice; it was my rebuke that made him ask for a divorce before he was discharged from the hospital. But my reprimand was a lie. I pretended that I was making it as a father, but actually it was only as president of Hoshijima Construction that I continued to blame him. In a roundabout manner, I kept implying that there was no choice for you two but to part. Yet I knew, in spite of all that had happened, that you didn't want to leave him. I'm sure you didn't. As your father, I understand that most of all."

I began to cry as I listened. He spoke without pause, then he suddenly stopped and became silent for some time. In that long silence I listened to my own sobbing as I sat in the living room, now aglow with the setting winter sunlight.

"That may be, but the horse's front legs were broken, the jar had been shattered. Isn't that right, Father? Isn't that what you said in the coffee shop at Arashiyama before Arima and I parted? But it wasn't really true at that time. It was after we parted—when I set my seal on the divorce papers—that

71

the horse's legs broke and the jar shattered."

At that point Father stood up, gesturing for me to stop: "Arima was a good man. I've come to like him." With that, he went to his own room with a ghastly expression on his face.

When Ikuko brought us tea and saw me sitting alone in the living room, sobbing like a baby with my head down, she seemed to be trying to think of something to say, but just kept silent. She set the teapot and cups on the table and returned to the kitchen without a word. Staring blankly at the steam rising from the spout of the teapot, I thought about Father's last words: "Arima was a good man. I've come to like him." Coming from someone who had been obsessed with work to the extent of ignoring his family and who distanced himself from others to the point of aloofness, these words somehow held conviction and great fondness. My former husband was indeed a good man. And now Father was sincerely concerned about my happiness. Those two thoughts gradually seeped into me like warm water. My hopeless, lingering regrets for you and my resentment toward Father suddenly vanished, and I felt as if I were floating in a pure white void.

When I came to, the sun had nearly sunk, and the moss-covered stone lantern in the garden had become a dark outline, its shadow stretched as far as the window of Father's room in the annex. After freshening up, I went to the kitchen. Ikuko told me that the day had been an auspicious one for her: her son, who would graduate from high school that year, had found a job. He had been hired by a famous French restaurant in Ashiya and would realize his dream of becoming a chef. The restaurant is called Maison de Roi. You and I went there two or three times.

Ikuko's husband died three years after their son was born. For about five years after that she lived with her in-laws on a farm in Tanba, but then she removed her name from her husband's family register and lived for a while with her older sister in Kobe's Higashinada Ward. My mother had died, and we were looking for a good-natured housekeeper. An acquaintance introduced her, and she began working for us as a live-in housekeeper, leaving her son with her sister. Ever since then, she's been like one of the family. She never said so, but Father and I thought that it must be painful for her to have to live apart from her only son, and we would sometimes ask her about it. We thought she should rent an apartment near Kôroen where she could live with her son and come to our house every day. But then you know what happened, so I hardly need write about it. Ikuko agreed with us, though just as she was looking for an apartment, the incident occurred. The incident itself didn't have anything to do with her, but she felt very sympathetic to me and began to show me as much concern as if she were my mother. She gave up looking for an apartment and announced that she would continue to work on a live-in basis. "I'll wait until after Aki feels better. After all, it's more convenient if I live here. I'm thinking that once my son has his career, I'll quit working and settle down with him. Boys don't need affection. Even he says that he doesn't need to live with his mother at this stage in his life." Then she lowered her voice and added, "If you had to take care of your father, you'd have a nervous breakdown. Leave it to me."

From that time on, there was no longer any talk of her getting an apartment and coming in to work. Ikuko's way of taking care of things would make you think she had been around Father for decades; she takes no notice of his tantrums or his willfulness in dealing with people, but humors him and never makes him angry. I have always admired her and been grateful to her. Whenever Father's visits to Tokyo turn out to be lengthy, he often takes Ikuko along, which shows how much he trusts her.

Upon hearing that her son had found employment and would be apprenticed at Maison de Roi, I commented that someday his skills would be sought after by French restaurants throughout Japan. She was worried whether he had enough perseverance, but she couldn't conceal her joy, and the way she used the kitchen knife and arranged the food on the dishes was more rhythmical than usual. When I said that he was lucky to have found a job in such a prestigious establishment, she responded, "Your father put in a good word for him. He wrote a note, and when my son took it to the interview, he was hired on the spot."

Ikuko briskly continued cooking, humming all the while. I went to Father's room. He was sitting on the floor in front of a low desk, writing. When I thanked him on behalf of Ikuko's son, he turned and replied gruffly that there was no reason to thank him. "Father!" I cried out, and that instant my tears started trickling down again. He looked at me and asked if I had come to his room just to cry. Then, stuffing what appeared to be a finished letter into an envelope, he smiled for the first time and said, "So why don't you go abroad then? A change of scene is the best thing to change one's mood."

74

"There's no need for that. I have already forgotten about the incident."

Facing his desk, Father just said "Oh?" without looking at me, and then remained silent. I crouched behind him, wrapped my arms around his neck, pressed my cheek against his back, and whispered, "I truly have forgotten. Truly!" But the more I said it, the more I saw your face before me.

Stroking my arms with his hands, Father muttered, as if to himself, "People change. We're strange creatures that go on changing minute by minute and hour by hour." Then he added, "You're a sweet girl, and I'm sure you'll find happiness." Central to the countless unforgettable memories in the ten or so years since we parted, the commanding ring in Father's voice then—along with the chill in the air in that deathly silent, unheated eight-mat Japanese-style room—have for some reason remained quietly alive.

Not only did I not go abroad, but after that I didn't even venture as far as the shopping districts in Kobe or Umeda. Around the end of the cherry-blossom season, when all kinds of trees were bursting into leaf, the rebuilding of Mozart was completed. Although the owners had fire insurance, the price of lumber had risen nearly forty percent since the time of the original construction, and the owners had to go heavily into debt. The coffee shop was rebuilt to look exactly the same as before, but for financial reasons a cheaper wood was used, so on the day that it reopened it seemed different. Nevertheless, as I walked in, at least Mozart's music remained unchanged. It was the Fortieth Symphony, which I liked better than the Forty-first, the Jupiter. After congratulating

75

the couple on the reopening of their shop, I took my usual seat at the table facing the street.

"Your coffee cup broke so we found a nice one for you at a china shop in the Kawaramachi district of Kyoto."

The owner placed the new coffee cup in front of me. It was an undecorated, light gray cup with a coarse texture, and was so thin as to be nearly translucent. It looked very expensive, and I asked to be allowed to pay for it. He insisted that it was a gift and, despite my urging, would not tell me how much it cost.

It was a Sunday, with many people strolling along the street under the cherry trees with their new leaves. The shop was filled almost to capacity, and for the first time in months I was enjoying a good cup of coffee while listening to Mozart. It was then that I noticed Father, who was taking a walk. In a cardigan and sandals, he seemed to be enjoying the mild sunshine as he strolled toward the shop. I poked my head out the door and called him inside. He sat down at my table and asked how the coffee was. He believed that the coffee served in a small specialty shop near his office in Yodoyabashi was the best in Japan. The owner, overhearing that, approached and said that the coffee in his shop was the second-best in Japan. Realizing that it was my father, the owner's wife also rushed over, her cheerful smile showing that her good spirits had been fully restored. She thanked Father profusely for the consolation money and said she hoped he would continue to favor them with his patronage.

I knew that when Father had no social gatherings, he would go straight home, and so I never imagined that when he left the office at the regular hour one day, he would have his driver park in front of Mozart and enjoy a cup of coffee before coming home. After that occasion, he would sometimes return home on foot. Even if Ikuko asked what had happened to the car, he would just say that he had been dropped off near the highway and had walked back. On such days he would always eat dinner later than the rest of us. I found this suspicious and pressed him for an explanation. He laughed rather shamefacedly and said, "I've been using your coffee cup."

"I can't believe you've been listening to Mozart!"

In response to my astonishment, he looked somewhat pensive and said, "I've been discussing your marriage prospects with the coffee shop owner."

I gave him a startled look and said, "I have no wish to remarry." I spoke in a decisive manner, because I knew he always got his way in everything and would not yield easily. Moreover, Father was the sort who rarely joked. What he said was as follows:

"Actually, there is a man who has taken a liking to you. The other day, Mozart's owner sounded me out in a roundabout way. It's his nephew. He's a lecturer at the university. He's thirty-three but still single. His specialization is Far Eastern history, and they say that he's sure to be made an assistant professor in a couple of years or so. Apparently, he has only met you once, at his uncle's condominium, but since then he has seen you at your table when he sits at the counter. It would be his first marriage, but he doesn't mind that you were married before. He's devoted all his time to his studies and hasn't come across any suitable marriage partner, but when he saw you he took an immediate liking to you. That's what I was told. When Mozart's owner first brought the matter up, I wasn't too enthusiastic, but he was so eager that I agreed to meet the man once. I asked the owner not to reveal that I was your father and just had him introduce me to the young man casually, as a regular patron. We didn't talk about anything serious, just things like: 'The weather has turned nice, hasn't it?' 'About how much do college lecturers make?' 'What sort of field is Far Eastern history?'

"I'm no longer considering having my son-in-law take over the company. I gave up on that completely when you and Arima Yasuaki parted. And choosing a different successor isn't something I can do. When I retire from Hoshijima Construction, someone suitable will take my place—I've come to terms with this. My chief concern is you and your happiness. Think about it. You've just turned twenty-six, and your life is about to begin. As long as you find a good person, the proper course is for you to get remarried and start a new family. If you don't like this man, you can simply refuse without worrying about it. Be that as it may, I think that at least you shouldn't object to meeting and talking to him."

In his peculiar, high-handed manner, Father was actually urging me to agree to a formal meeting with the man. As I listened, I thought, "Oh yes, that man," but for the life of me I could not recall his features or his personality. To be sure, when I heard he was a lecturer, I thought, "Yes, he did have that air about him," so he must have had distinctive features. And yet, no matter what Father said, I was not ready to agree to a formal meeting. After all, you had not receded from my mind, though there was absolutely no way I could expect you back. Smoking one cigarette after another, Father continued talking.

"Today I stopped by Mozart again and talked to the owner. I told him the whole truth behind your divorce and asked him to convey this to his nephew. I didn't care about his reaction, but after hearing me out he looked downcast and was lost in thought for some time. Then he said that he felt the marriage proposal could not reach a happy conclusion. He thought you would still need time on your own. He said, too, that he had sensed you had undoubtedly experienced profound grief. Otherwise, there was no way that someone so young could have been able to unravel the secret of Mozart's music so quickly and more perceptively than him. Then he bowed and asked that we forget about the marriage proposal, though it had come from his side. I asked why, but he said nothing. Then I found myself making a counterproposal.

"The divorce was not the result of my daughter's infidelity but her husband's, and it was unavoidable because of the attendant tragedy. The divorce itself didn't seem like sufficient reason to abandon the proposal. The way I spoke betrayed a mild irritation at the owner's reaction. I added that I hadn't actually wanted to give my daughter to some underpaid, unknown college instructor. The owner apologized politely for his rudeness, but wondered aloud whether you had really wanted to part from your husband, in spite of the incident. For an instant I felt as if a hole had been bored straight through me. He added that when he remembered you distractedly sipping your coffee, he couldn't help wondering if that might not be the case. Then he repeated what he had said earlier, about you needing a good deal of time, and it occurred to me that it might well be true. But then the opposite thought came to me: Yes, but for that very reason, shouldn't I help her find a suitable person so she can rebuild her life? I said this aloud, and the owner again sank back into his thoughts. He seemed to have changed his mind, and asked whether or not I had told you about this discussion. When I replied that I had not yet broached the topic of marriage with you, he suggested that I do so that evening, that unexpected things do happen, that you might like his nephew, and that the two of you might turn out to be a very happy couple. This time, I was the one to fold my arms in thought. The type of man I like least is one whose appearance is shabby. Next to that is someone who can't hold his liquor. My impression from having met him once was that Katsunuma Sôichirô was neither of these. He seemed to have a rather nervous temperament, which is not uncommon of a scholar, but on the whole he had a clean feel about him. And so I'm doing what the owner suggested and am bringing the matter up with you."

I had never once won an argument with Father, and that occasion was no exception. After hearing him out, I asked him to let me think about it and went upstairs to my bedroom. I stood by the upstairs window. The quiet residential neighborhood was bathed in the bluish tint of a wintry night. A nearly full moon had risen. Not having achieved perfect roundness, it looked distorted somehow. It occurred to me that a year had passed since we parted, but it actually felt more like three or four years. It was as if the oppressive weight of an incurable fatigue had settled on my mind and body. It was a fatigue that resisted relief no matter how much I rested, no matter how strenuously I worked, and no matter how much I indulged in pleasurable distractions. I tried to imagine what you would be feeling and concluded that you weren't likely to have been able to forget me completely after only one year. My husband had been snatched away by a woman I didn't know, but I was still flattering myself. I immersed myself in all kinds of fancies, but forced myself to the conclusion that, even if you had not forgotten me, you must have given up on us, and I decided that I ought to do likewise. I should have done it a year earlier, but I was not able to. "I must give up." I repeated these words to myself over and over, followed by what Father had said: "People change. We're strange creatures that go on changing minute by minute and hour by hour." How would I change? Thinking about that made me tremble with anxiety. Again I was overcome by the premonition that something unfortunate was about to begin—both for you and for me.

On a Sunday two weeks after that, the coffee shop owners, Katsunuma Sôichirô, Father, and I met for dinner at Maison de Roi. Mr. Katsunuma, Father, and I were rather quiet, and Mozart's owner and his wife anxiously attempted to introduce topics of conversation. After dinner the others returned home, while Katsunuma and I walked to Ashiyagawa Station on the Hankyû Line and stopped at a coffee shop.

"My uncle told me the details of your divorce." Katsunuma tried to think of what to say next but was unable to find the right words. He frowned as if mildly irritated, alternately stroking and tugging at his sideburns, so I offered the conclusion I had come to.

"I'm still not ready to get married again. I don't have anything in particular planned for the future, but I would like to wait longer."

Katsunuma looked directly at me and immediately said, "Then I'll wait, too."

There was nothing about him that put me off, but there was also nothing about him that disposed me favorably toward him. We spent the evening in desultory talk, and after leaving the coffee shop just after nine he saw me home in a cab. Even now, I'm not sure why I decided to marry him. Perhaps the best way to describe it is this: if getting divorced from you was like being forced to get on a boat that was pulling away from the jetty, then marrying Katsunuma was like finding myself on a boat without any desire to go anywhere. The extraordinary thoughtfulness of the couple from Mozart influenced my decision—not to mention Father's fervent wish for my happiness—but beyond that there was the need to forget you once and for all.

Katsunuma Sôichirô and I were married in September of that year. Father wanted to adopt him into the Hoshijima family as heir, but had to abandon that because Katsunuma was an only child who was living with his mother and whose father had died when he was in college. He could not very well leave his mother living alone, much less consider adoption into the Hoshijima family, so I ended up marrying into the Katsunuma family. Thus, even though things did not turn out quite the way Father had hoped,

82

he nevertheless pressed on with the marriage arrangements and never expressed his thoughts on the matter.

The Katsunumas lived in an old two-story house with a small garden in the Yuminoki district of Mikage. It may have been different had it been a second marriage for both of us, but since it was my husband's first, Father put up the money for a proper reception and wanted us to go on a honeymoon. In fact, he was annoyingly insistent on an overseas trip, and I followed his wishes like a lifeless doll. My honeymoon with you was a short and simple trip to the northeast, wasn't it? If we had wanted to go abroad somewhere, Father would probably have handed over the money straight away, but you and I opted for a tour through the northeast in winter. I wanted to visit Europe—Paris, the Netherlands, Rome, and so on—but you wanted to see the northeast in the winter, and nothing would dissuade you. It started snowing hard when we were traveling to Towada from Lake Tazawa, remember? So we changed plans and spent a night at Nyûtô hot springs. That night we sipped hot local saké as we listened to the flurry of snowflakes falling thick and fast. That night I began to love you with all my heart. Though I had been in your arms many times, long before our marriage, in bed with you at that small inn in Nyûtô I got to know you more deeply. What stupid things I've ended up writing again! I'm embarrassed in spite of myself. Allow me to return to what I was talking about.

Following Father's wishes, Katsunuma and I took a tour through the countries of Europe. Not a month had passed after I returned to live with Katsunuma and his sixty-seven-year-old mother when something totally unexpected occurred. Returning home after shopping at the neighborhood market, I found my mother-in-law lying on the kitchen floor. I immediately called an ambulance, but she died not long after reaching the hospital. It was a myocardial infarction, and not much could be done for her. On the forty-ninth day after her death, when the Buddhist services were concluded, Father urged Katsunuma to move into the Kôroen house. He was reluctant at first but finally gave into Father's persistence. Thus, after barely two months of living away from home, I again took up residence in Father's house.

It's now just past three in the afternoon, and before long I'll need to go and pick up Kiyotaka. I've spent days writing this long letter, but I haven't been able to put down half of what I want to say. It seems that I'll be pestering you with more letters, even if you tear them up and throw them in the garbage unopened.

The bus from the school for the handicapped arrives in front of the station at three thirty, so I have to hurry. I'll end this here and begin another letter. This is an abrupt way to conclude, but I hope you stay well.

Yours sincerely,
Aki

July 31

Dear Aki,

I didn't tear up and throw away the two letters I received from you. In fact, I read them. To be quite honest, when I received mail from you two months after I had asked you to stop communicating with me, I put the thick envelope in my desk drawer and left it there unopened for two or three days. I was going to neither read it nor respond. But in the end I couldn't resist the silent signals emanating from the envelope. I wanted to read it after all, so I opened it. As I read your letter, I realized how much you have changed during these ten years. I can't really put into words how you have changed or what has changed about you, but you aren't the same person I knew. You have struggled for eight years to bring up a handicapped child (I sense that "struggled" would be the most apt word). It occurs to me that, as a person, you are definitely stronger and better rounded than before. This may be a trite way of putting it, but in the process of raising such a child there must have been countless times when you had to grit your teeth against the anguish and hardship that an outsider could never understand. What would it have been like if we had remained together and had such a child? When I think about this I wish I could make it up to you for what happened ten years ago, all the unhappiness I caused you. When I'm drunk at the counter of some bar in a run-down part of town, or when I look blankly at the posters hanging in a crowded, swaying train, I am beset by an irrepressible feeling of penitence that threatens to tear me apart.

But I didn't pick up my pen to write such craven thoughts. There was one word in your letter to which I simply must respond to. You wrote that listening to Mozart for some reason conjured up the word *death*, and you said to the owner of the coffee shop: "Perhaps living and dying are the same thing." After finishing your letter, I went back and reread that passage again and again. I was overtaken by an impulse to relate a singular experience. This, too, is likely to be a long letter, but I will only write down what I saw, without including any of my own speculations or inferences. But to preface this story I'll begin with the day I ran into you on Mount Zaô.

Why did I go to Zaô Hot Spring that day? It's a simple story that begins with a bizarre incident. The business a friend and I had started wasn't going well, and a promissory note I had issued out of desperation fell into the hands of a shady character. It was an invalid note that I had issued out of necessity, with the intention of immediately redeeming it. But a miscreant had gotten hold of it and was going to use it as a source of income, so I was forced to come up with a sizable amount of money by the due date. I headed for Tokyo and spent about a week running around, asking friends and clients for help, but I failed to raise the money. I was in a state of panic. Near Iidabashi Station, I glanced back and saw a young man watching me. He was neatly dressed, but there was something about him that revealed he was of the same mold as the reprobate who had my note. Since my company consisted of only myself and my friend, they must have interpreted my going to Tokyo as an attempt to escape and had followed me there.

I ducked through the crowd and jumped on a train that had just pulled in, but then the man rushed up, pried apart the doors that had begun to close, and also boarded the train. Now that I think about it, I might have only been deluding myself. It's possible that he was just a bystander, that somehow our eyes met, and that by coincidence he jumped on the same train I was on. Nevertheless, I was determined to get away from him somehow. It seemed that he kept turning around to look at me. I got off at Ochanomizu Station; he followed. So I decided to take a train to Tokyo Station and give him the slip. As soon as I reached Tokyo Station, I ran down the stairs at full speed, and without giving any thought to where I was going, dashed onto another platform and hid at one end of it. The man was nowhere to be seen. A train stopped and I got on without knowing where it was headed. It soon arrived at Ueno Station. I decided to disappear for a while—anywhere would do. I just wanted to vanish for two or three days. Even at the ticket counter I kept looking around nervously, but there was no trace of the man.

I have no idea why I bought a ticket for Yamagata, but as I took the bills out of my pocket, I found myself saying, "One ticket for Yamagata, please." I looked at the signboard announcing arrivals and departures and realized that the Tsubasa No. 5 express train would leave in five minutes. Again I raced down the platform and stopped in front of one of the car doors, this time looking around carefully. I couldn't see the man anywhere. The train began moving, and I arrived in Yamagata a few hours later, in the evening. Of those who got off, I was the last in line at the ticket gate, and once I was through I regained my composure. I had only sixty thousand yen in my pocket, not a great deal after deducting the cost of a return ticket to Osaka. Looking for a cheap inn, I walked through the shopping district in front of the station to the bus terminal for Mount Zaô. Zaô's a busy ski resort in the winter, but surely there would be inexpensive lodges available during the off-season. I thought of hiding out there for three or four days, contacting my friend in Osaka, and planning my next move.

To tell the truth, in the ten years since we parted, I've made my living in disparate ways. Really disparate! It would take two or three years just to write down everything about each job. People speak of declines, but in these ten years I have experienced a slow, steady fall. Come to think of it, it began a year or so after our marriage, when I went into the department store in Kyoto's Kawaramachi district to buy a melon and, recalling Yukako with sudden longing, went up to the bedding section on the sixth floor to see her. Then my descent began. In these ten years, I've worked for more than ten companies and tried my hand at all sorts of businesses. I have had relations with numerous women, one of whom supported me for three years. I'm living with a woman now. She is kindhearted and takes good care of a good-for-nothing, but I feel no affection for her. I could describe these ten years by using a sumo analogy: If I push my opponent backward, then I get thrown out of the ring; if I thrust, then my opponent dodges; if I try throwing my opponent down, then I am thrown over; if I attempt to throw my opponent by hooking his leg from the outside, then I am brought down by a hook from the inside. No matter what I try, it ends up backfiring. It's as if I were being haunted by some evil spirit. When I ran into you at Zaô, I was at my lowest point.

When I arrived at the hot-spring resort, I walked up the gentle slope, which reeked of sulfur. Inns lined both sides of the road, but with my meager funds I couldn't stay in any of them. I inquired at a tobacconist's if there were any small lodges near the top of the mountain and was told that there were some next to Dokko Pond. I walked up the path leading to the gondola platform next to the dahlia garden, got on the gondola, and went up to Dokko Pond. There were some buildings there that appeared to be what I was looking for. I entered one and asked about the cost for a two- or three-day stay. The price was even lower than I had expected, and, relieved, I sat down on a dirty bench inside. Since it was the off-season and I was the only guest, they couldn't offer much, they said, and would only serve what they had on hand for meals. I agreed to their terms and went upstairs to a room that, in the winter, would be packed with young people. The youthful owner explained that the second story would then become the entrance because the first floor would be buried under more than four meters of snow.

The building was too large to be called a "mountain lodge"; there was a shop and a dining room on the first floor, while the second floor had rooms with beds. I was told that if I wanted a hot-spring bath, I could take the lift down to the inn area, where

I would find an inexpensive municipal bathhouse. I had an early supper and took the lift down the mountain. After soaking in the sulfurous water of the public bath halfway along the road, I had a cup of coffee in a small shop and returned to the lodge by Dokko Pond. As you wrote in your first letter, no moon or stars were out that night. I crawled into bed at about eight o'clock and slept like a log. Indeed, I was a man who was just like a fallen, rotten log.

The next morning, after breakfast, I wanted a cup of coffee and took the lift down to the coffee shop I had been to the previous night. I was just going to hang around until noon, but then I realized I had to contact my friend in Osaka. I thought of using the telephone in the coffee shop, but reasoned that, as joint manager of the company, my friend was likely dashing about trying to raise money just as I was, and might even be running away from some thug. If he was also in hiding, then there was only one place he could be. Although he was a married man with children, there was a woman with whom he was on intimate terms. But the notebook containing her phone number was in the little travel bag in the upstairs room of the lodge. I rushed back to the dahlia garden and hurriedly jumped on a crowded gondola, though in terms of time it would have made little difference if I had waited for the next one. And it was there that I ran into you, of all people!

My surprise when I saw the tastefully dressed woman sitting opposite me may have been even greater than you sensed. I was unshaven, my shoes and shirt collar were dirty, and my complexion was far from healthy. Anyone would have been able to tell at a glance what my situation was. I lost all my composure and could think only of vanishing from your sight as quickly as possible. As soon as I got off the lift, I hurried to the lodge without a backward glance for old times' sake. I dashed straight upstairs and, hiding by the window, watched as you and your son on crutches slowly passed. Even after you had left the trees behind, turned right onto the mountain path, and disappeared from view, I stood transfixed for a long time, looking in the direction where you both had gone. On the path, the dappled patches of light filtering through the trees were transformed—in a way I have never experienced before—into desolate daggers that lacerated my sullied heart. I forgot all about calling my friend and just leaned against the window frame for ages, waiting until you and your son came back around the bend and through the trees. A few hours later, when I saw you coming through the patches of sunlight, something like boiling water welled up from deep inside me. Aki had become the wife of another man and a mother, and appeared both well-off and in good spirits, I thought. You were totally unaware I was watching you from the second story as you made your way as slowly as before, disappearing down a small path through the trees toward the gondola landing stage.

There were no other guests in the lodge that night either. The owner, who was about my age, brought me a kerosene heater. He tossed out several interesting topics in an attempt to make conversation, but seeing no change in my expression, he went downstairs after reminding me to turn the heater off before going to bed. I think it was about nine o'clock, probably when you and your son were looking at the stars in the garden. I turned off the overhead fluorescent light, switched on a small reading lamp, and lay down on the futon. The sound of the trees by the pond swaying in the wind was mixed with snatches of cheerful banter between the owner and his wife downstairs. Occasionally, something hard would hit the windowpane. It wasn't a moth but a kind of beetle. For a while I closed my eyes and breathed in the odor of the humid room, where the various sounds combined to produce an unsettling silence. The smell was oddly familiar. Then I heard a strange noise coming from a corner of the room. I sat up and peered in the direction of the sound.

Two blue jewels were glinting in the dark. A cat was arching its back and edging slowly toward something. As my eyes grew accustomed to the dimness, I was able to make out the cat's size and color, as well as a red cloth collar around its neck, which meant that it must belong to the family. I seized a pillow and was just about to throw it to scare the cat away when I noticed a mouse cowering motionless in the opposite corner of the room, facing the cat. Only once, when I was a child—I must have been six or seven—did I watch a cat eat a mouse. One hardly sees this anymore, so I kept my eyes fixed on the two animals to see what would happen. The cat paid absolutely no attention to me but took a step forward with its ears pricked, then waited for its next move with an amazing degree of attentiveness. In that fashion it approached the mouse a few inches at a time. I glanced around the room to see if the mouse had anyplace to escape, but the door was firmly shut and the window was locked, with the curtain drawn. There didn't seem to be any way out for the mouse. On the ceiling, I spotted a hole right above the crouching mouse. If it raced up the wall that instant, it could get away through the hole.

But the cat pounced. The mouse was as defenseless as if it had been tied up. The cat sank its front claws into the mouse's back and only then looked at me, its eyes narrowed into slits. It was a look of triumph. And then the cat began to play, tossing the mouse into the air. After the mouse had done a somersault in midair and tumbled to the floor, it tried to run away for the first time, but was easily captured and tossed up again. This was repeated several times. The cat's supple movements had a certain innocence, as if it were playing with a ball or something. As I watched the interplay between the two, it didn't seem like the final minutes of an encounter between a killer and a victim, but rather like a friendly romp between two creatures who had let their guards down. The cat flung the mouse up a dozen times, and when the mouse stopped moving and just lay where it fell, the cat rolled it over with its paw, first onto its right side and then onto its left. Finally, the cat looked at me with an expression of utter boredom.

"Just leave it alone now." As soon as I mentally uttered those words, the cat began to gnaw at the mouse's belly. Still alive, the mouse was disappearing bit by bit. When its head stopped jerking and its limbs ceased to twitch, the cat lapped up the blood that had spilled onto the tatami and continued to eat the tiny dead creature, including its bones. I could hear the crunching sound made by its skull, which the cat had saved for last. After licking up all the blood, the cat began carefully cleaning around its mouth with its front paws. Only the tail of the mouse, apparently not to the cat's liking, remained on the tatami. Suddenly I was filled with an urge to kill the cat. A mysterious hatred welled up within me. Near the door was an empty vase. I quietly rose, picked up the vase, and approached the cat, which was still licking its mouth. When the cat saw me, the hairs on its back stood on end, and it raced toward the door. It had understood my intentions. "You think you're going to get away?" I thought to myself. "There's no way out." However, to the side of the door was a gap in the wall large enough for a fair-sized dog to pass through, let alone a cat. It had been disguised with a board on the other side, so I hadn't noticed it. But the cat knew it was there and, knocking the board aside, made its escape with ease.

Sitting on the futon, I smoked a cigarette and stared at the tail of the mouse. I'm not sure how much time passed, but after several cigarettes I finally put out the last one and lay down. The many questions that had plagued me during those ten years again arose persistently in my mind. What kind of woman was Yukako? Why did she cut her throat with a knife? Didn't I perhaps treat her the way that cat treated the mouse? Or was it Yukako who was like the cat? In order to explain the background to my thoughts, I would need to write about several incidents that occurred between Yukako and myself, but I think I'll save that for another time.

I didn't sleep a wink that night, but continued to think as I lay under the quilt. The image of the mouse being eaten alive put me in an agitated state of mind. I thought of many things—you walking past my window in your purple outfit; the years that had passed between our getting acquainted and getting divorced; the dead Yukako; my brief time in Maizuru; the promissory note I had issued; the money I needed to raise…. Thinking about these things in various ways, I suddenly realized something: wasn't I myself both the cat and the mouse? Among the many mental states generated throughout my life, I observed the cat and the mouse, now living, now dying. And then it occurred to me: that day I must have drifted into the realm of the dead and had a glimpse of my own existence.

That day. That day ten years ago when the tragedy occurred. I have decided to record it as accurately as my memory allows.

After finishing work at the office, I headed for Kyoto in a company car. A certain private college in Kyoto planned to commemorate the centenary of its founding by building a library and a memorial hall, and several construction companies were submitting bids. It wasn't a project that had particularly interested our company, but when Tanikawa Contractors gave an absurdly low estimate, as if to say, "There's no way we're going to let Hoshijima Construction get this," your father ordered me, in his usual terse, autocratic style of speaking: "Land the job." As the person in charge of the project, I contacted the college president and chairman of the board of directors with an introduction from a professor with whom I was acquainted. Leaving business details aside for the moment, when I suggested to them that we dine together somewhere quiet where we could relax, they agreed, so I took them to the Fukumura restaurant in the Gion. The college people were already quite tipsy by the time we finished our meal, and as both the president and the chairman of the board were elderly, I gave up the idea of going elsewhere for a second round and took them straight to their homes. Since I had already made reservations at Club Arles for after-dinner drinks, I had the driver pull over at a public phone on the road, and I called to say that we had changed our plans and would not be going there.

Ordinarily, I would simply have taken a cab to the Kiyonoya Inn in Arashiyama, where I would have waited for Yukako to come after finishing her shift. But Yukako, who answered my call, said she didn't want to come that night. I asked why, but she wouldn't answer. Then it hit me: it was the man who stopped by her bar every day. He was the manager of a large hospital, fifty-two or fifty-three years of age, with a fine build. For three months he had been trying to win her over with promises that he would set her up in her own bar. When I heard about his proposal from Yukako, I said that, as long as she was going to make a life for herself in the world of late-night entertainment, it was not a bad offer. And I really meant it. I didn't expect my relationship with her to last long, and was rather of a mind that I should put our affair behind us. On the other hand, I still harbored a lingering, deep-rooted attachment to her. I asked, "Are you going to see that man today?" Yukako didn't answer. I realized she would, and that she was free to do whatever she liked. I had no right to interfere. But jealousy is a strange emotion. In an unusually angry tone, I said, "I'll be waiting for you at the Kiyonoya." With that I slammed down the receiver, sent the company car back, and took a cab to Arashiyama. I had a feeling that Yukako wouldn't come, but I waited anyway. At about three in the morning, she entered the room. Without a word she went into the bathroom and took a long shower. The Kiyonoya was an old inn, but they had rooms with baths for guests like us. The sight of Yukako's face as she sat next to me in her bathrobe gave me a start; it was the same Yukako who had sat half-reclining, with her wet hair hanging down that evening in Maizuru when we were in junior high school. I stared hard at her. When I parted her robe and began to move my hand up her thigh, she drew back and remained sitting upright. She had never refused me until that night.

"Did you sleep with him?" I asked.

"I'm sorry," she answered, giving me a piercing look. "Tomorrow morning, you'll leave and go home while I'm still asleep, won't you?" For a while we studied each other's face in silence. "You'll always go home, won't you, to your family? You'll never ever come home to me." This time she hung her head as she spoke.

"That guy, he'll go home to his family, too, won't he?"

Yukako gave a small nod, still looking down. I surprised myself with my own detachment, and I thought it was time for us to just break it off. I sat up and embraced her. I sensed that Yukako had been unfortunate from her early years. She was beautiful and possessed a unique sweetness, but this seemed to be the very cause of her unhappiness.

"Milk him for all he's worth, and let him shell out the money. He's loaded, isn't he? You have more to gain from him than by taking up with some no-good fellow. Get your own bar, work hard, and make lots of money."

Beyond saying things like this, there was nothing I could

do for her, but I did convey my honest feeling that I had loved her from the first day I met her in Maizuru, and that it was from her that I learned what love is. I told her that there was no way I could repay her, but at least she would never have to see me again.

Two emotions welled up inside me: jealousy and relief. The selfish prospect of relief at being able to part without a lot of trouble somehow endowed me with an attitude of patronizing generosity. When we got under the quilt, we just closed our eyes. For a long while I was unable to sleep, but I finally dropped off.

I woke up to a severe burning pain in my right chest. I saw Yukako sitting next to me, her long, slanting eyes blinking. She lunged over me, and I felt a sharp pain in my neck, as if I was scorched by a pair of red-hot tongs. I thrust her aside and stood up. Something sticky flowed down my neck and onto my chest, and the I recognized blood dripping onto the bedding. I flashed a look at Yukako's face before everything turned black.

According to the police, after Yukako stabbed me, she cut her own throat, about seven centimeters from the base of her right ear to her chin. The wound was three centimeters deep near the ear, where the knife plunged in with considerable force, but she must have weakened as she drew it toward her chin, where the cut was less than two millimeters deep. She collapsed into the tokonoma alcove and, according to the police, that was what saved my life. As she fell, her left arm knocked over the Kiyonoya telephone, which rings the front desk.

The owner was already asleep in his room, and the young employee on duty happened to be checking a faulty water heater in the large bathroom at the far end of the building and didn't hear the ringing. He returned to the desk about twenty minutes later, so the phone was ringing for at least ten or fifteen minutes, the police deduced. If the employee had worked any longer on the water heater, I would certainly have died, too. He picked up the phone, but there was no response at the other end. Thinking it strange that the receiver in the room was off the hook, he knocked on our door, but there was no answer. So he used a master key and entered the room. At that point Yukako was already dead, but I had a pulse and was still breathing. I don't know whether it occurred during the ensuing uproar at the inn or after my arrival at the hospital, but I slipped into a really strange mental state.

I think it was some time after I lost touch with what was going on that I felt a coldness gradually come over me. It was no ordinary coldness; it was as if my whole body were freezing, solidifying with a crackling sound. In that horrifying cold, I returned to my past. I can't think of a better way of putting it. All the things I had done turned into images that rushed around me at a ferocious pace. Despite the speed, each image was projected with great clarity. Enveloped in that eerie cold, I watched the images, but eventually I heard someone say, "There may be no hope for him." I remember the words clearly. After the images slowed down, I was assaulted by a pain that defies description. The images, devolving from my past actions, drew me into their midst. The past actions were composed of "good and evil." No other suitable phrase occurs to me, though it wasn't the good and evil of simplistic morality. I suppose you could say that a life-threatening toxin and its diametrical opposite—something pure—separated from each other and engulfed me.

I was able to see myself on the verge of death. Another self was observing the self that was making a reckoning of the good and evil it had done, even as it was being subjected to excruciating pain. People will likely say I was dreaming, but I was decidedly not dreaming; I was definitely observing myself, from a place slightly apart, in the hospital operating room. I even recall the surgeon's words. After I recovered, I asked him if he had said anything in the operating room. He cocked his head and asked with surprise, "Could you hear it?" It wasn't just that I'd heard it; I had definitely observed the entire scene, including the surgeons and nurses and the countless instruments in the operating room. The one who heard what the surgeon said was not the "I" lying on the operating table but the dying "I" that was off to one side, watching the other "I." It wasn't the self that was groaning in agony on the operating table, but another self that was observing everything.

Earlier I wrote that I was watching the self that was taking a reckoning of the good and evil it had done, even as it was being subjected to excruciating pain, but that's not so. As I write this now, delving into the deepest recesses of my memory, I should say I was also being forced to account for the good and evil of what I didn't actually do but only thought. So the self watching the dying me was tormented by a maddening anguish, a desolation, and an unaccountable remorse. I think I surely must have died for a brief moment. What was this other self? Could it have been my "life" itself, separated from my physical body?

After some time, the cold abruptly changed to warmth. The pain, desolation, and remorse all vanished, as did the other self. From that point until the moment I regained consciousness, everything was total blackness. I remember nothing. I heard a voice calling, "Mr. Arima, Mr. Arima," and in my blurred field of vision appeared the face of a middle-aged nurse. After a while, I saw you. I think you said something to me, didn't you? But I don't remember what it was. Then I fell asleep.

Whether anyone believes this or not, it is what I actually experienced ten years ago. Until today, I have never told anyone about this strange incident, and I intended never to tell anyone for the rest of my life. Yet when I read the words "perhaps living and dying are the same thing" in your letter, I became intrigued and thought about them at length. Perhaps the idea that life perishes with death is an enormous illusion created by arrogant human logic. I can't help thinking so. With my recovery, the "other self" that was observing me vanished. But if I had died, what would have become of that "other self"? Wouldn't it just have become a disembodied, spiritless "life," blending into the universe? And what's more, wouldn't it have continued in eternal agony, bearing all the good and evil of my actions? I repeat that what I saw was definitely not a dream. On the contrary, it was, if anything, the "reality of life" itself.

I began writing this by declaring that I wasn't going to include my own speculations or inferences. Yet I must admit that I haven't been able to avoid inserting a few interpretations based on my speculations. I have often wondered if that "other self" might not be what is commonly called a "spirit." I don't understand what a "spirit" is supposed to be, or if it really exists. But no matter how I think of it, what was looking at my dying self—or, rather, at the self that was nearly dead—was not my spirit. If it were, then I would have to suppose that even while we are alive, our physical and mental activities are ruled by this thing, this "spirit." In that case, not only our bodies—our heartbeat, circulation, the hundreds of hormones, and the incredible functioning of our organs—but also the ceaseless, infinite changes in our minds would all be controlled by a "spirit." But we are not like this. Our bodies function independently; we laugh, cry, and become angry of our own accord. Our lives do not move according to the dictates of a "spirit." I have come to the conclusion that the "other self" is only a repository of my actions—good and evil—which continue to exist after death, and are subjected to endless torment. It is not the ghost that is often called a "spirit" but rather the "life" within us, which, while allowing us to feel anger, sadness, joy, and pain, also allows complex and subtle physical and mental activities. It wasn't anything like a "spirit." It was definitely life, which ultimately cannot be expressed through color or shape, much less through words. Such were my thoughts as I gazed out the hospital window during my convalescence and saw the signs of approaching spring.

I was completely unable to forget this eerie experience, and I became frightened to go on living. I may have survived, yet the day will surely come when I'll face death. I'll be placed in a casket and hauled to a crematorium. I'll vanish from this world without trace. But my "life," cloaked in the mantle of good and evil with which I have been burdened, will live on. This very thought made me shudder. The odor of Yukako's body as I embraced her that fateful night returned, and I envisioned her childlike demeanor as she nodded compliantly at everything I said.

I killed her. This fact is rooted in my mind. But as I had such an unforgettable glimpse of my own life, the experience had to transform me. "I must live differently from before," I thought, as my wounds healed. I realized how much hurt and grief I had caused you, my wife. My love for you continued to grow and deepen after the incident, to a greater degree than before. At the same time, it was accompanied by a powerful and tormented affection for Yukako.

It was at that moment that your father, Hoshijima Teruta-ka, hinted that he thought we should divorce. His manner of speaking was unusually roundabout, but insistent all the same. Had I not had that strange experience, I would probably have bowed my head and pleaded for another chance to live as a couple, provided you were agreeable. But I was moved by the thought that I had to change, that I had to live differently from before. On the evening when I was given my discharge date from the hospital, I put an end to my vacillation and decided to divorce you. I supposed that I would then be able to face a new life.

To be sure, I did change and try to live differently. But, instead, I sank to the lowest depths and turned into a haggard, lackluster being, weary of living. As I watched the cat eat the mouse in my room at Zaô, you were sitting on a bench in the dahlia garden, gazing at the stars in the night sky with your handicapped son, weren't you? It's possible that the three of us were actually seeing the same thing, in separate places. How strange it all is! And how fraught with sadness is this life! No, I shouldn't have written that. I think I'll end my letter here. If I keep on writing like this, I'll reveal things better left unsaid. Please take good care of yourself and keep well. Enticed by your profound words about Mozart's music, I ended up writing about something that I was never going to tell anyone as long as I lived. I have let myself go on self-indulgently, but please dismiss this as the ramblings of a lout who was nearly killed by a barmaid.

Regards,
Yasuaki

P.S. Regarding the sender's name, I couldn't very well write "Arima Yasuaki" on a letter addressed to you, since you have built a new home life, so I made up a woman's name. I'm sure you recognized the sender as soon as you saw the handwriting.

August 3

Dear Yasuaki,

I wept as I read your letter. I couldn't stop the tears. To think that you were upstairs in the lodge next to Dokko Pond watching us as we passed! And to think you waited hours by the window until we returned along the shady path by the pond! How could I have known? I don't have the slightest idea what I should write, my eyes still are brimming with tears. I "appeared both well-off and in good spirits." Why did you have to say this? To be sure, you could have said that I'm better off than the average housewife and I'm not suffering from any ailment. But you didn't say, "Aki looked happy." I know very well that you wouldn't dare write anything like this.

You saw through me, didn't you? And so you remained by the window for hours, waiting for my return along the path in front of the lodge, in order to verify what you had seen about me. I'm sure of it. The story about your strange experience took me by surprise. When I finished reading your letter, my mind went blank, and I waited for some time until my feelings calmed down. Then I reread the section about what you felt and saw when you were dead. I read it over and over. It was beyond my understanding. You used the phrase "good and evil" to describe your past actions. But what exactly is this "evil" you speak of? And what is the "good"? These words I cannot possibly comprehend. All I understand is that you didn't make this story up, and that you did have the experience you described. And yet I'm not sure how to respond. Perhaps it would be best not to refer to your letter for now and just keep the strange experience you related locked away in my heart.

I am very grateful you read my two long letters and even replied to them. I feel certain that you will write again. My intuition tells me so. The thought that you will again be reading my letter and responding makes me very happy, but at the same time I have an uneasy feeling that I am somehow defying morality. This confession will no doubt elicit a wry smile from you, but our correspondence (assuming you respond to this) must someday come to an end, which I fully acknowledge.

Today I am feeling terribly on edge, and nothing comes to mind as I try to write. It would make sense, then, just to wait a few days until I've calmed down, but when I received your letter yesterday, I had an irrepressible desire to respond immediately. Until recently, my husband was away in America and I had more time to myself. But since his return I have again been busy with domestic chores. On top of this, after my husband left this morning, Kiyotaka shut himself in his room and refused to go to school. When I asked why, he just stuck out his lower lip in a pout—his usual sign of strong dissatisfaction—and lay curled up in bed, not saying a word. Something must have happened at school. Since he is unable to express himself well, he presumes on my indulgence whenever something is troubling him. When I'm firm with him and scold him in the mornings, Father, already in his suit as he waits for the company car to pick him up, says, "If he doesn't want to go, he doesn't have to. Let him do as he pleases." It's always the same: an argument with Father who insists that since Kiyotaka is handicapped, I ought to treat him more leniently, though I feel this is precisely why I should not give in to his whining or indulge him.

We didn't know Kiyotaka had a congenital disorder until about three months after his first birthday. He couldn't sit up or crawl, he had little or no facial expressions, and his reactions to noise and motion were slow. When he was about nine months old, I sensed something wasn't quite right and wondered if he might have an abnormality, but I was afraid my suspicions would prove correct, so I put off taking him to the hospital. One book I read on child-raising said that some children will sit up at five months while others will be unable to even after eight months, so I tried to convince myself that Kiyotaka was just behind. But when he was still unable to sit up three months after his first birthday, I could no longer deceive myself, and I was horrified. "Judging from the firmness of the muscles, his is a mild case, but it is unquestionably congenital cerebral palsy." After the doctor's diagnosis, I somehow made it home holding Kiyotaka in my arms, though I don't recall how, or what route I took.

Until Ikuko came into my room that evening with a worried look on her face, I remained sitting on the floor next to the baby bed, holding Kiyotaka against my breast, staring vacantly at the carpet. I was overcome by shock and grief, and I had lost my normal presence of mind. But when I got up in the middle of the night to change his diaper, the thought struck me: I hadn't done anything wrong. Why did I deserve this? Then I looked at the face of my husband as he lay asleep, and another unexpected thought flashed through my mind: if this child had been born to me and Arima Yasuaki, he might have come into the world with a sound body.

What a terrifying idea! And what contempt for my husband! Still, I seriously entertained the thought. Kiyotaka was the product of Katsunuma Sôichirô and myself. If I had not married Katsunuma, I would not have had Kiyotaka. It was all the fault of one man: Arima Yasuaki. It was he who forced me to have this pitiable child. As I sat there in the dim light, my features must have turned into those of a diabolical ogre. Mentally I was screaming, "I'll never forgive Arima Yasuaki. Never, never, never! It's his fault! His fault!" As Kiyotaka grew and his handicap became more evident, my hatred for you intensified.

Ah, I am really too worked up now! My hands are shaking, and the strength has left my fingers. My mental turmoil from reading your letter has combined with my agitation from having horrifying feelings of malice toward you, and now I can't make sense of anything. Please forgive me. I suppose I really ought to end here for tonight. Even if you don't respond, I'll write again. The tears have started again. I wonder why I am so weepy this evening. What's wrong with me?

Sincerely,
Aki

August 8

Dear Aki,

When I saw how cramped and shaky your usually fine hand was—
and that near the end of the letter it became strangely chaotic and
distorted—I went to a cheap bar behind the station that I haven't
been to in a long time, sat down at the counter, and drank alone
until the place closed.

It has been ages since I drank so hard. With a heavy heart
and some self-contempt, I thought as I drank, "I see. According to
syllogistic logic, I am definitely responsible for Aki having a child
with a congenital handicap." I couldn't help wallowing in the
gloomy thought that the fate of so many people was linked to my
casual visit to the bedding section on the sixth floor of a Kyoto
department store—or, going further back to junior high school
days, getting off at East Maizuru Station to become the adopted
son of the Ogatas after my parents' died. It's exactly as you say: I
was the one who had brought all of this about. And I have been
continually punished for it during these ten years.

I was resigned to the fact that there was no other way to
see it, and I downed an enormous amount of whiskey, more than
I realized. Now and then the bar owner, who is my age, would
come over and talk to me, but I made no reply and only stared at
the contents of my glass. The regulars at this cheap bar were:

former *yakuza* now employed at local pinball joints; sullen workers from small local factories; and delinquents who had no regular employment but supported themselves with any odd job they could find, using their earnings to bet on bicycle and boat races. You would think that once in a while someone a bit more respectable might drop in for a drink, but the usual crowd never included such people. Puffing away at cigarettes, the customers made passes at the owner's young wife (they kept their marital status secret, but I knew they were a couple immediately), offered lewd comments, and laughed exaggeratedly at stupid jokes. Most didn't leave until the place closed.

I wrote in a previous letter that after I was tossed into the sea in Maizuru that November day and Yukako jumped in after me, we went to her house looking like a pair of drowned rats. Then, after we had changed and faced each other over a small heater in her upstairs room, Yukako, with a forwardness far beyond her fourteen years, rubbed her cheek against mine and covered my face with kisses. I'm sure I added these words: "The ability of a fourteen-year-old girl to act toward a boy like that, without reservations, no doubt revealed Seo Yukako's karma." As I became more inebriated, those words drifted into mind. Though I had written "karma" myself, I pondered for a long time, wondering what this could possibly mean.

As I evoked the feel of Yukako's body, I vaguely began to understand the true nature of what clung so strongly to the other self observing my dying self. It seemed more than my past actions because things which had not yet found expression in acts, even the congealing of what had been mere thoughts—spite, anger, affection, and foolishness—became plainly etched into my "life," branding me with a mark for all eternity and chastising me as I moved into the world of the dead. This gradually became associated with the word *karma*, which entered my mind the instant I thought of Yukako. Without understanding how or why the two were related, I realized they definitely merged at some point. However, as I became very drunk, the cheap purple lighting in the bar and the rows of whiskey bottles turned into a blur and started to spin. I had difficulty breathing. I don't know how much time passed before I felt someone behind me shaking my shoulders. In a stupor, I turned and stared dully at the woman standing there. Reiko, the person I'm living with, was worried and came to collect me. She also apparently paid my tab.

Standing up unsteadily, I stumbled outside. I felt inferior to a dog that was standing by the side of the road. A few people who had gotten off a train passed me, each vanishing in a different direction. Every one of them seemed superior to me. The image of you and your son as I watched you from the lodge at Dokko Pond appeared in my mind. I felt like a worn shoe tossed into a ditch. Reiko was following a little behind me, not saying a word. I was too drunk to be articulate, but I was fully conscious. As I walked along, I became nauseated. I bent over, my face almost touching the ground, and expelled the contents of my stomach. Reiko rubbed my back and said she would wipe me down with a cold towel when we got back to her apartment. Shaking free of her, I hurled out some hateful words: "I can't stand you! It gives you pleasure, doesn't it, to devote yourself to a man like me. You come to the bar to get me, looking all worried. Without my asking, you pay my bill. You follow a few steps behind, pretending to give me space and to leave me alone. What role are you playing in this one-person drama of yours? My puking fits right in, doesn't it? You rub my back and want to wipe me down with a cold towel when we get home. Even as you talk, you're really obsessed with your womanly virtue and kindness. But I can't stand you. I don't feel anything for you. If we split up this minute, I'd feel no pain or regret."

Reiko stared at me, looking both bewildered and innocent. She was at a loss how to respond, like a young schoolgirl suddenly scolded by a teacher for no apparent reason. Then, in a detached voice, she said, "I've never thought of getting you to marry me."

Feeling oddly disconcerted by what she said, I retorted, "Then let's separate. I'll move out tomorrow."

Reiko is twenty-eight. I met her a year ago. I was her first man, so she had no intimate knowledge of men until she was twenty-seven. She had begun working at a large supermarket after finishing high school and, except for her days off, has stood at the cash register every day to this day, punching in codes and prices. She has done the same job for nearly ten years, and now her only pleasure is to pack a lunch and drag me out for a picnic on Thursdays, her day off. She isn't interested in fancy cuisine; she doesn't think of saving up for a trip to Hawaii or Guam; and she doesn't spend much on clothes. She is small, her complexion is as fair as that of a young girl, and in the way she moves her large round eyes there is still something of the purity of a girl approaching puberty. She doesn't care for useless chatter, and if you could call reticence that I occasionally find irritating a saving grace, then this is to her credit.

Reiko is the second of six children. Her elder sister, married to a man who earns a meager salary, maintains a very ordinary household. After graduating from high school, her two good-for-nothing younger brothers neither worked nor continued their studies, but disappeared for months on end. When they did come back, it was only to filch money from their parents before running off again. Her two younger sisters are still in high school but rarely attend. Instead, they put on gaudy makeup and gad about the amusement quarters. Her father is a carpenter, but he hurt his back on a job and hasn't been able to work much. That was twelve or thirteen years ago, and with no income from him since, they depend on the slim wages her mother takes home from a small factory, and on what Reiko and her elder sister send them each month. This is what Reiko told me. I have never met her siblings or parents.

When we got to the apartment, I undressed and collapsed onto the futon Reiko spread out for me. I felt hot and asked her to turn on the air-conditioner, but she said that cold air was not good for someone who was drunk. She poured water into a basin, fetched ice cubes from the refrigerator, and dipped a towel in the water. After wringing it out thoroughly, she began wiping my body. Without a word, she rubbed me all over with the cold towel: forehead, face, behind my ears, neck, chest, stomach, and back. After she finished, she sat with her legs tucked under her and looked at my bare body for a long time. Then she traced the scars on my neck and chest with her fingertip. I had never said anything to her about them, and she had never asked. Her silence about them made me rather uncomfortable. This was the first time she had touched my scars. It felt good while she was wiping my body, but afterward I was even hotter. I asked, "Can you please wipe me down again? It felt really good." Reiko complied. As she did so, I said, "It's late. Let's go to sleep."

The hands of the clock pointed to two in the morning, and Reiko always got up before seven to prepare breakfast and leave for work at eight thirty. She answered dispiritedly, "I won't be going to work tomorrow." Then she stared at the scar on my neck again. She said that she had accumulated a lot of paid vacation so there would be no problem taking two or three days off. This was the first time since we started living together that she planned to take any of her paid vacation. I must have really upset her with my heartless words.

Once more I told her that we should separate, then I closed my eyes, vaguely thinking Reiko might do the same thing to me that Yukako had done. Strange, isn't it? Even though I've changed so much from ten years ago, I end up acting the same way.

For some reason, I was in a quiet and composed mood. Reiko turned off the lights, changed into her pajamas, spread her futon out next to mine and lay down on her stomach, then rolled over to face me. In a subdued, barely audible voice at first, but then with increasing passion and eloquence, she related the following story.

"My grandmother died when she was seventy-five. I was eighteen at the time. I remember my youngest sister wasn't even in kindergarten yet. The day of the funeral was cold and rainy. Unlike my brothers and sisters, I was so close to Grandmother that everyone in the neighborhood kidded me about it, and I can't help feeling she also showered me with special affection. Grandmother always used to conceal her left hand—tucked into a sleeve when she was wearing a kimono, or into a pocket when she had an apron on. She was born without a pinkie on that hand, a rare birth defect. When she was a child, the local kids always used to tease her. She had five sons, four of whom she lost in the war. They all died in battle about a month before the war ended, at nearly the same time but in different places—Burma, Saipan, Leyte. When I was young, Grandmother used to sit me down in front of her and tell me how much she had cried when reports of her sons' deaths suddenly arrived, one after the other, in such a short period of time. No matter what she started out talking about, she never failed to end with this story. When I was small, I may have been a better listener than my brothers and sisters, and no matter how many times she repeated it, I always listened with unfeigned interest, while massaging one earlobe between my thumb and index finger. This has been a habit of mine since I was very young, and because of it one ear always feels hot and flushed. Sometimes, even now, I catch myself at work massaging my earlobe with one hand while punching buttons on the register with the other. Whenever I realize it, I quickly lower my hand.

"When she had finished talking, Grandmother would always

show me her deformed left hand. She would also add that not one of those powerful people who lived at a safe distance from the battlefields and who sent men off to war would be reborn as a human being. Neither was there any difference between the powerful men in the victorious country and those in the vanquished country. They were sure to be reborn as snakes, earthworms, centipedes, and other loathsome creatures. Even if any chanced to be reborn as human beings, they would be suitably punished for the sin of having driven people to their deaths, and would thus lead short, miserable lives. When Grandmother said this, her face always grew tense, and even to my youthful eyes she appeared resolute. She believed in reincarnation—that people who died would necessarily be reborn. As proof, she would show me, her young audience, her left hand with only four fingers, and say, 'Look at this weird hand.'

"Even now, I don't quite understand why she made me study her deformity, but she would say, 'These fingers have made me realize one thing. My four sons were rounded up and sent away, and the war ended soon after they died, one after another, in lands far to the south. Nearly a year after, when I was almost fifty-one, I was walking through the burned-out ruins of Osaka in the heat, wondering why my sons had to die so young, when it suddenly struck me: Maybe I'll meet them again somewhere. No, I'll definitely meet them, and not in a future life but in this one. I'll be able to meet three of my dear sons. I cried from both a joy and a sadness that I can't describe. I pulled my four-fingered hand out of the pocket of my work trousers and held it up to the sunlight.

I stopped and stared at the creepy thing for a long time. Even to me, it was so ugly and frightening that it made me shudder. And yet that four-fingered deformity somehow made me realize I would definitely meet my sons again in this life.'

"I always had to listen to her story. To me, it was like a fairy tale, but I always sat up straight with my legs properly tucked under me and listened, constantly massaging my earlobe, until Grandmother grew tired. But there was always something I found strange: even though four of her sons had died in the war, why did she think she would meet only three of them in this life? I never asked her but would just listen in silence. Like a set phrase, Grandmother always concluded her story with this admonition: 'Taking a life is the most wicked thing anyone can do. And not just another person's life—taking your own life is just as bad. There are plenty of bad things in the world, things you shouldn't do, but these two are the most horrible and wicked.' It was many years later, shortly before Grandmother died when I was in high school, that I found the answer to the mystery. She said her four sons had died in battle, but this was not entirely true. My father said there was at least one untruth in Grandmother's story. Three of her sons did in fact perish in battle, but the second-eldest, Kensuke, seeing his comrades die one after the other from starvation and malarial fever in Burma, walked deep into the forest and hanged himself. His death in battle had been fabricated by the military, and Grandmother learned the truth from a soldier who had been repatriated from Burma. He came to visit, carrying a small square paper box containing Kensuke's ashes, as well as his glasses and his tattered notebook. When Grandmother heard that Kensuke had not died by an enemy bullet but by his own hand, her face turned deathly pale. Only one thing was written in his notebook: 'I was not happy.'

"On the day of Grandmother's funeral, after the cremation, Mother and I were bustling between our cramped kitchen and the parlor, throwing together a modest repast for relatives who had traveled from afar. Suddenly I remembered her story, and I wondered if she had met her reborn sons somewhere during her lifetime. As I served beer and saké to the guests, I thought she most likely did not. Yet oddly enough, at the same time I also felt she may have met her dead sons somewhere after all without realizing they were her sons—and without their realizing she was their mother. They must have exchanged glances somewhere, if only for an instant. With this thought, I was overwhelmed by intense feelings of profound joy and sorrow, and I felt like bursting into tears. No doubt the fatigue of the wake and the funeral had put me in an unusually sentimental and delicate state of mind. I was able to understand what Grandmother meant about meeting three sons in this life, not four. She was sure she could never meet Kensuke, who had committed suicide, and thus would not be reborn as a human being. I felt I understood her thinking. All four were her children and precious to her. They were all taken off to war, and not one returned. But I would venture a guess that of the four, the one she actually most wanted to see again was Kensuke. I'm sure she cherished Kensuke in her heart as her dearest and most pitiable child."

When Reiko finished talking, she nestled her face against my side. I was surprised, and spontaneously put an arm around her shoulder. It was the first time she had ever talked so much of her own accord, and also the first time she had taken the initiative in cuddling up to me. But I only asked her brusquely what point she was trying to make. Perhaps exhausted by so much talking, Reiko let out a deep sigh, and said, "I have this feeling that you're going to die." I gruffly asked why I would die. Reiko started to say something, but caught herself and stopped.

I closed my eyes as I wondered what she was trying to tell me by relating a story about her grandmother. The four-fingered hand flashed before my eyes like something I had actually seen; and the words left by the young Kensuke who had ended his life in a Burmese jungle, "I was not happy," kept running through my head until it seemed I would never get to sleep. I whispered to Reiko that I wanted her to take off her pajamas. Sitting up on the futon, I made Reiko—now compliantly naked—assume a position she found most humiliating, and had my way with her. I hurriedly squeezed out what had accumulated within me, then pushed away from her immediately, falling onto the bed. Then, with my back to her, I pretended to snore. After some time, Reiko began talking again. "I have a good idea," she said, rubbing her cheek against my back. I pretended not to notice. I was experiencing that unpleasant sobering up after drinking too much, and I wanted to get right to sleep. Reiko again spoke quietly: "I wonder why Grandmother didn't tell me that one of her four sons died by suicide instead of in battle." I, too, wondered why, but I didn't feel like saying anything. I didn't really care one way or the other. Eventually, I fell asleep.

I woke up late the next morning. Several pieces of paper were spread out on the small kitchen table, and Reiko was writing something, lost in thought. When I asked what she was doing, she smiled and repeated what she had said the night before: "I have a good idea." After I washed my face, I sat down opposite her and lit a cigarette for my morning smoke.

Reiko was covering pieces of paper with tiny numbers, and drawing rectangles in which she was writing notes. With her eyes fixed on one of those pieces of paper, she asked me, "How much money do you think I've saved up?" Actually, I had secretly taken a peek at her savings bankbook, which she kept stowed away under the clothing in her chest of drawers, but I answered that I had no idea and asked her to pour me a glass of cold barley tea. Ordinarily, she would do so immediately, but her eyes were glued to the bits of paper, and she pointed at the refrigerator and said, "It's in there. Pour it yourself." There was no use arguing, so I opened the refrigerator, whereupon Reiko announced, "I have 3.2 million yen." She finally looked up from her papers and smiled at me with a cheery expression that concealed some kind of scheme: "I also have a million yen in a certificate of deposit that will mature on the third of next month." If she hadn't been sending her father money, she would have saved more, but if she and her elder sister didn't help out, her parents wouldn't be able to get by on just her mother's earnings. "So it can't be helped," she explained, as if to apologize.

I mumbled, "You make it sound as if you've been saving that money just for me." She shot back angrily that she had no such intention. I laughed, saying that I was only joking, and she answered with a hint of mirth in her big round eyes, "I got to know you only a year ago. I couldn't very well have saved 4.2 million yen in that time."

Then she began to talk about a business she had been thinking of starting. The idea had occurred to her when she went to her beauty shop. Lately, there has been a lot of competition among such shops. In a single city block there might be as many as five or six —in some cases even ten—each vying for customers. They all work hard to keep up with the latest trends and provide the best service to their customers, but their biggest headache is advertising.

She explained, "The beauty shop I go to makes something like a monthly brochure that it hands out to customers. But it isn't as if thousands of copies are printed, so the price per copy ends up high. And besides, it's a bother to make a new one each month. Lately they've been ordering them from a small design studio, but production costs are rising. When the beauty shop owner told me this, I got an idea."

Reiko showed me what she had written. A sheet of paper was folded in two like an advertising brochure. On the top of the first page was a rectangle in which was written the name of a shop and its manager, as well as the address and telephone number. Beside that was the name of the brochure in large lettering—a provisional name, because she had not decided on anything yet. Reiko said that on the first page she would also put things like photographs of seasonal flowers to represent the month. She unfolded the sheet to show the second and third pages, which would feature an article on such things as the proper way to shampoo hair at home, advice on skin care, recipes for novel dishes, and illustrations of popular hair styles. She said that she was still considering what to put on the fourth page, the back.

Reiko's eyes were radiant. As she tapped the rectangle on the front page with the tip of her ballpoint pen, she leaned forward and said, "This is the beauty of the whole thing. Everything can stay the same, except for the shop's name and the manager's name." She kept talking while I listened, not saying a word. She had recently visited a small printing shop nearby and inquired how much it would cost per copy. For thirty thousand copies, they would be able to print it in two-color for seven or eight yen a copy. Assuming she could sell them to shops in batches of two hundred for four thousand yen—and that with thirty thousand copies she could get a hundred and fifty shops as customers—then she would be in business. At twenty yen a copy, four thousand yen per month would be like an advertising fee for a shop, with an attractive brochure thrown in with its name, phone number, and any other wording they wanted. Beauty shops would welcome it. With a clientele of a hundred and fifty shops, sales would total 600,000 yen. At seven yen a copy, the printing cost would come to 210,000 yen. Even allowing for various overhead costs, the profit would be half the total sales, or 300,000 yen.

I didn't quite follow her idea the first time, so I asked her to repeat it. She obliged with even more enthusiasm. I asked how the writing in the blank space would be printed, thinking that, depending on the number of orders, it might be necessary to reset the type as many as a hundred and fifty times for thirty thousand copies. If that were the case, they wouldn't be able to produce them for seven or eight yen apiece.

"No, it's not like that. The space would be left blank on the first printing of all thirty thousand copies. Then type would be set separately for the lettering inside it. All thirty thousand copies would be printed once more, two hundred copies at a time."

"Can they really do that?"

"The printer gave me his word," she answered with a laugh.

"But so what if it's cheap advertising at twenty yen a copy? If every shop is distributing the same brochure, they'll think twice about it. When they realize that everyone gets basically the same brochure, with the only difference being the name and telephone number of the shop, customers won't be very interested in it, will they?"

"That's why I'll keep a strict system of making contracts with only one shop per neighborhood. The sales point of this business is that once I've signed a contract with one shop, I won't ever sign up another shop in same territory," Reiko answered, brimming with confidence. "And," she added, "eighteen shops have already asked for the service."

Without my knowing anything about it, Reiko had put together a rough sample and negotiated with the beauty shop she goes to. The owner was enthusiastic about the idea and said that if she could have a brochure with different contents each month for twenty yen per copy, then she would be happy to sign a contract. What's more, she had even recommended it to friends who had opened beauty shops in Kyoto and Kobe. Those friends had recommended it to others in the same business in different areas, and before she knew it Reiko had promises of contracts with eighteen shops.

"But that's still only eighteen shops, isn't it? If you have 30,000 copies printed but contracts with only eighteen shops, what will you do with the other 26,400 copies? You'll pay 210,000 yen to the printer, with only 72,000 yen coming in," I said.

Lining up her savings bankbook and the soon-to-mature certificate of deposit on the table as evidence, Reiko explained, "At first, I'll operate at a loss. But once my clientele has increased to fifty shops, I'll break even, and when I have a hundred and fifty shops, I'll be clearing a profit of 300,000 yen. If I try hard and get contracts with three hundred shops, I'll have a monthly income of 600,000 yen. At that rate I could branch out to Tokyo, Nagoya, and even expand into the countryside. It could reach a thousand shops, or even fifteen hundred." Reiko's idea grew bigger and bigger.

"If you limit yourself to one shop per area, you'll be covering a larger territory as your clientele grows. How are you going to find more contracts?" I asked.

Without the slightest hesitation, she said, "You'll travel around to different shops."

I stared at her in amazement for some time. Still dumbfounded, I asked, "And who is going to plan each month's brochure?"

"You'll do that, too." Reiko looked me squarely in the face, then covered her mouth with both hands to suppress her giggles.

"Well, make me some coffee and toast. I haven't had breakfast yet."

Reiko finally stood up. I think she's gone off the deep end, I thought to myself, feeling uneasy. What she was saying wasn't just reckless. In the year I've known her, Reiko has never once revealed her own ideas or feelings. I never knew what she was thinking, and I only noticed her reticence and gentle disposition. She is no beauty, and you couldn't call her particularly intelligent. Such was my impression of her. But with her loquaciousness the night before and her plans this morning, I can only say that she seems like a completely different person.

Reiko watched me with her big, dark eyes as I chewed the toast. "Yesterday, I believe I said we should part," I threw out coldly.

She fixed her gaze on my chest and began intently kneading her earlobe with her fingers. "I don't want you to talk anymore about parting." She was already crying before she finished speaking, and asked, "If you leave me, what will you do?"

I answered that I hadn't thought that far ahead. Since I didn't really feel like leaving her just then, I was satisfied that she had been reduced to tears. It was pathetic of me, but if I had left her, I wouldn't have been able to support myself. And I just wanted to hear from her own lips that she didn't want to separate. That's why the night before and again in the morning I had tormented her with my insistence that we split up.

I told Reiko that I no longer had any desire to try my hand

at a new business. It didn't matter what potential it might have, once I got involved, it would end in failure as it always has. I had had enough of business. Death had already cast its shadow over me. If she wanted to do this, she would have to do it herself.

How selfish, I thought, amazed at myself as I looked at her large, moist eyes. I myself do nothing except try to be taken care of by a woman. And still I manage to keep sinking.

It was past noon when we left the apartment and went to a coffee shop in the neighborhood. Reiko, who seemed in low spirits, said, "I won't ask you to do any work. Just help me out a bit. To begin with, before I can start selling, I need to have a sample ready. So my first priority is to make a brochure for the eighteen shops I've already got an agreement with. But I don't know what kind of articles would be good for the second page, or what topic should go on the third page, and I can't think of what to do with page four. And so, just this once, I'd like you to think of something. Then, when this turns into a real business, I'll need to think up a name for the company, and I'll need a prospectus and a leaflet to mail directly to beauty shops in areas around Osaka. Won't you please at least help with this?" Reiko pressed her hands together in supplication.

Feeling wearied by the whole thing, I asked, "Don't you care about losing the 4.2 million yen you've worked so hard to save in a worthless business venture?"

She answered, "This is sure to turn out well. If it doesn't, I can always go back to the supermarket, can't I?"

At any rate, she already had contracts with eighteen shops.

She needed to deliver the first brochures by the end of August, and it was already the fifth. The printer needed the finished text and photographs by the tenth, which meant that we had only five days left. I wondered whether I could put together such a brochure in just five days when I've had almost no experience at this sort of thing. But seeing Reiko's desperate expression, I ended up answering, in spite of myself, "Just this once." About four years earlier, I had worked at a reputable, medium-size printing company. I quit after three months, but as a salesman I had been in charge of selling a brochure for an old Japanese confectionery shop in Shinsaibashi, and I felt that I'd be able to come up with a good layout somehow. However, that brochure had been created by the company's designers and copywriters, and it wasn't as if I had made any direct contribution.

Reiko's face suddenly brightened. We hurriedly left the coffee shop, and she took me to a bookstore in front of the station, telling me to buy anything I needed to design the brochure. While I was looking for books, she went to a stationery store and bought several sheets of art paper, a ruler, compass, glue, erasers, and whatever else she could think of. I picked up a copy of *Shiatsu You Can Do at Home* and a book titled *Home Vegetable Gardening*. I also bought a thick volume titled *Encyclopedia of Fascinating Miscellanea*, another called *A Manual of Ceremonial Occasions*, and two monthly beauty magazines. The situation was desperate. In five days I not only had to put together a brochure—which I've never done before—but it also had to appeal enough to beauty shop managers that they'd want to subscribe. So I have to end this letter here.

Reiko has been taking time off work ever since, and has been running around all day to beauty shops and to the printer. It's time I started on the brochure. I've spent three days on this letter, so only two days are left. But since she has taken care of me for a year, this is the least I can do in return. Right now I have the books I bought lined up in front of me, along with a scenic photograph that could be used for the front page, pencils, a ruler, and the art paper. The photograph is one taken on our honeymoon, on the shore of Lake Tazawa. It's the one photo still among my belongings. You never know what will prove useful, do you? I thought this would be an incoherent letter, bouncing all over the place, but as I read it over, I think it's a pretty accurate record of events from the time I received your letter until today.

Sincerely,
Yasuaki

August 18

Dear Yasuaki,

Ikuko took your letter out of our mailbox and brought it to me in the kitchen. Suppressing a giggle, she said, "What cute names your friends have!" When I saw the sender's name, I, too, ended up laughing. "Iris Garden," of all things! It sounds like the stage name of a star at the Takarazuka all-female song-and-dance troupe! Your previous letter was addressed from "Lily LaFleur." If you don't use a little more ingenuity, my family will become suspicious.

I opened your letter late at night, after my husband and Kiyotaka had both gone to bed. I recall something I wrote in reply to the letter in which you shamelessly told of your chance meeting with Yukako in Maizuru. I poured my anger into those words, demanding that you tell me all of the particulars of what happened between you and Yukako up to the very end since I had a right to know. Then I doubled my attack by adding that I wouldn't be satisfied until I knew all the romantic details. (You see, I was so furious when I read that letter I wanted to tear it into pieces.) But now I no longer care about the details. In your third letter—the one where you recounted your strange experience—you fully described what went on between you and Yukako. You wrote very simply about your last night with her, but on rereading your letter the other day, I realized that everything about the two of you—from

your meeting in the Kyoto department store to the incident itself—
is implied. It is sufficient enough for me, though.

"You'll always go home, won't you, to your family?"
Yukako's words assuaged the tension that had built up within me.
I felt something akin to affection toward her. "Affection" is perhaps not the right word. She was a woman who had stolen my
husband, but, as another woman, I felt that I wanted to console
her, that I could face her calmly and with tranquility. I now sometimes feel as if she were very familiar to me, though she will never
come back. And yet, buried somewhere in my heart, jealousy has
taken firm root. The story of Reiko's grandmother I cannot dismiss as a mere fairy tale. There seems to be a frightening truth in
what Reiko's grandmother said, that someone who takes the life
of another—or, as with her son, his own life—will not be reborn
as a human being. Even I thought it strange that a story bordering
on a fairy tale should ring so true. Sitting in the bath or watering
the bushes in the garden at dusk, I would wonder why her grandmother's words should weigh so heavily on my mind. I finally realized it is because I am the mother of a child like Kiyotaka. Kiyotaka was born with a defect, albeit a different one, just as the
grandmother. Though his is a mild case, he definitely came into
this life bearing a burden of unhappiness. Why did my son have
to be born with such a burden? Why did Reiko's grandmother have
only four fingers on one hand? Why are some people dark-skinned?
Why are some born Japanese? Why don't snakes have legs? Why
are crows black and swans white? Why are some people blessed
with health and others cursed with infirmities? Why are some born

130

beautiful and others homely? As Kiyotaka's mother, I want to know the real reason for the unfairness and discrimination that are stark realities in this world. But no matter how much you think about such things, nothing ever comes of it. Yet as I read your letter I was absorbed in such thoughts. Suppose the grandmother's words weren't just something to be laughed off, but were actually true…

When you referred to Yukako, you used the word *karma* and said it was connected to the congealing of "good and evil," which clung stubbornly to the other self that was watching you die. Ah, I no longer understand what's what! I'll try to bring some order to my thoughts. To do so, I'll have to touch on my relationship with Katsunuma Sôichirô, something I've not written about before.

Katsunuma doesn't drink, has no interest in golf or tennis, doesn't gamble, and knows nothing about go or shôgi. What's more, to him, Mozart's music is only so much irritating noise. I thought the only thing that could move him was some abstruse historical document. Three years after our marriage—one year after Kiyotaka was born—Katsunuma was promoted from lecturer to assistant professor. Even before then his students would occasionally come to the house, but after he became assistant professor, their numbers suddenly increased. There were both men and women, most of whom were in the seminars he conducted. Among them was a beautiful, tall, and slender woman who had a certain aloofness about her. She always seemed intentionally standoffish, as if conscious of her own attractiveness and proud of it, and I never warmed to her. One day, several students visited as usual, talking excitedly. Feeling quite at home, they helped themselves to beer, juice, and cheese from the refrigerator, surrounding Katsunuma with their clamor. Toward evening, all the students left together. When they were thanking us as we saw them to the door, that woman looked at Katsunuma and smiled faintly. She was communicating something secret with her eyes. I stole a glance at Katsunuma's face and was shocked. He, in turn, was conveying something to her with his eyes. I immediately became aware of the relationship between them. At that point it was no more than a premonition, but my premonitions, as you know, often prove correct.

About two or three months later, Father's secretary, Okabe, brought us two large sea bream he had caught in Wakayama. (I'm sure you remember Okabe's fondness for fishing.) We decided to keep one ourselves and give the other to Mozart's owners, who were now my relatives. I wrapped the fish in wax paper and set out. Ordinarily, I would go down the street, turn right at the second intersection, and walk along the river, but a large stray dog with its tongue hanging out was standing in the way. It scared me and I retraced my steps to make a long detour through a dark street I rarely take. Walking along, I saw Katsunuma and the young woman embracing in the shadow of the gate of a large house. I hurried back the way I had come and cautiously went past the stray dog to the coffee shop. I gave the owners the fish and then returned home.

Katsunuma didn't come home until late. He and the student had been in each other's arms right in our neighborhood, but they must have gone somewhere afterward. Perhaps they went to the beach on the far side of the tennis courts or to the "love hotel" behind the station. I wasn't saddened in the least, nor was I shocked. I greeted Katsunuma as if nothing had happened, and he acted likewise. I thought, "What foolishness! How sordid they had looked!" Katsunuma's relationship with that student was both vulgar and dirty, but at the same time I was hit by the sober realization that he wasn't important to me. I had not married him out of love, and even after several years I didn't feel anything remotely like affection for him. I told myself that I didn't care, and that I had Kiyotaka, a dear, dear child who was born into the world with a burden of unhappiness. I felt convinced that I would be able to continue to live for him alone.

Seven years have now passed, and the affair between the student, who has since graduated, and Katsunuma is still going on. I know about it but have never said anything. Sometimes the scene of my husband and that vixen embracing in the dark alley flashes through my mind. They don't really appear as human beings but rather as something filthy, like soot in human form, and then the image instantly vanishes. When Katsunuma would occasionally reach for me in bed, I would invent an excuse such as, "I think Kiyotaka is saying something. I'd better see how he is," or "Kiyotaka was a real handful today and I'm exhausted," or something to that effect, and I would refuse to let him have his way. But I don't want to write any more about this. People would surely be surprised to know that since the day I saw Katsunuma and his student embracing, we have never made love. Not once in seven years. Eventually it dawned on him that I knew. Not that he said anything, but I could tell he knew. On the surface, though, we pretend that nothing is amiss, and have lived together in this way until now.

I think I have come to understand the meaning of the word *karma*. Not just as a word but as a stern sort of law. No matter whom I marry, my karma is such that another woman takes my husband away. Even if I left Katsunuma and married someone else, I think the same thing would happen again. When I read the passage in your letter where you used "karma" to describe a congealing of good and evil clinging to life itself, it occurred to me that losing you—and Katsunuma's affections shifting to another woman—might all be the workings of my karma. Perhaps it's just my own egotism that leads me to suppose this. Before I talk about karma, I should probably reflect on my own existence as a woman. I guess there must be something lacking in me, as a woman and as a wife. Is it sex appeal? Am I not submissive enough? You know, don't you? Please feel free to tell me.

It seems that Father has just come back. This time he stayed in Tokyo a good while. He must be tired. He, too, has been aware for several years that Katsunuma has someone else. I didn't tell him, but Father is the sort of person who can see through other people. I'll write again. Oh, I almost forgot to mention it, but it made me quite nostalgic to read the abuse you hurled at Reiko when you were drunk. Back when we were lovers, we often quarreled about silly things, didn't we? Predictably you would end by saying, "I can't stand you!" But my high opinion of myself would make me think, "Hah! You're really madly in love with me," and I would become excessively spiteful. "I can't stand you!" Reiko is the sort of woman who can make you say such things, isn't she?

Yours sincerely,
Aki

September 10

Dear Aki,

Let me begin by answering your question. Speaking as someone who knows you, I can say you are a most attractive woman, and your attractiveness never changed either when we were lovers or after we were married. Even in bed, while you hadn't mastered all the tricks of a prostitute, you were sweet and sometimes did your best to be adventurous, and you put up with the humiliation of accommodating my willful demands to assume some demeaning position. You were more than sufficiently pleasing. Had you possessed any more sex appeal, you would have made a husband a bit uneasy. Moreover, I recall you being very compliant. And that's not just flattery; I really mean it. You had a pampered upbringing, and possessed enough of a willful streak that I wanted to slap you at times, but for the most part if I stroked your head and said, "That's alright," you quickly turned obliging, so even your willfulness became part of your charm.

However, this is all as I knew you, and I can't claim to know how things have been with your new husband. Male infidelity is like an instinct from which there is no escape. Most men are just built this way. "What a self-serving excuse!" women will say indignantly—but it's true and it can't be helped. Even if a man has a beautiful wife whom he loves, if an opportunity comes his way, he

136

will most likely sleep with another woman. But that doesn't mean anything has changed in his affection for his wife. But no, I can't really state any such conclusion. Let me revise what I just wrote. Some men do fall for other women and abandon their families, but usually a man's infidelity is just the type of thing I'm describing. If I write any more, it will turn into an egotistical defense of my own behavior, so I'll stop here.

At any rate, I've been working for the first time in a long while, and I'm dead tired. What's more, it's not always pleasant. For two days I hardly slept while I was working on the brochure. Otherwise I couldn't have finished it in time. In our rush, we decided to call it *Beauty Club*. What a stupid name! But we couldn't think of anything else, and if we didn't give it some name, we couldn't proceed. On the second page I followed what Reiko had on her sample and wrote a special feature on the right way to shampoo your hair. The third page I filled with descriptions of different types of shiatsu, altering the wording of what was in *Shiatsu You Can Do at Home*. If I made the descriptions any closer than they appeared in the book, I would be charged for blatant plagiarism. I agonized over what to put on the fourth page, but couldn't come up with a single good idea. Finally, thinking "What the hell," I rearranged some intriguing stories from around the world appearing in *Encyclopedia of Fascinating Miscellanea*, and added two or three puzzles and riddles from books I had recently purchased. After putting all this together, I had to discuss the layout with the printer.

Before the brochures were ready, Reiko borrowed a small

car and asked me to drive. I have a license but haven't driven for nearly five years. Reiko, armed with a map of Osaka and five or six offprints the printer had given us as samples, said, "Let's go!" She mentioned that she had decided to plead with the printer to print only twenty thousand copies this time. Since the price per copy would go up to ten yen, she explained, the payment from eighteen beauty shops wouldn't amount to much and so we needed to find at least a few more shops willing to sign contracts before the end of the month, when the brochures were to be delivered.

We concentrated on Osaka's Ikuno Ward. When we found our first beauty shop, Reiko had me stop the car while she went inside. She was in there for a full hour, and just when I assumed that she must have sealed a contract, she came out, saying, "No deal." At the next shop, she was tossed out in two minutes flat. We went to five shops in all and didn't get a single contract. The heat was ferocious that day, and the rattletrap of a car we were using didn't have air conditioning.

Dripping with perspiration, I leaned against the burning seat and said, "Please, I've had enough!" But Reiko dug her heels in: "We're not going home until we get at least one contract." After lunch at a cheap restaurant, she put the car keys in my hand again and said, "Let's go!" When I asked to rest a bit longer, saying that driving right after a meal is bad for the digestion, she answered, "OK, I'll get you some cold coffee." We moved to a coffee shop next door, but even before the coffee arrived at our table she began to urge me to hurry up and drink it. When I deliberately took my time, she focused her large, round eyes on my chest and muttered miserably, "You're being perverse. Here I am putting my heart and soul into this, and you won't get serious."

"Whether I'm 'serious' about it or not, I did what you asked me to do, and have been doing exactly as you tell me, haven't I? I went two days without sleep to get this brochure ready, and I was the one who went to explain the layout to the printer. Plus, I've been running around this sweltering town today, driving this rattletrap you borrowed, which just belches smoke and doesn't build up any speed. I'm the one who's being worked like a horse and yet I've stifled the urge to complain." At this retort, Reiko's despondent face broke into a smile, and her dark eyes began to dart about. Suddenly amused, she laughed, wrinkling her round nose. (Her round nose surely disqualifies her from being called a beauty, but it does have the merit of conveying an innocent, affable charm.)

When I asked what was so funny, she replied, "I've been keeping you for a whole year for moments just like this." Then she covered her mouth with both hands and couldn't stop laughing. At first I was furious, but before I knew it I was laughing, too. She's got me, I thought.

When I asked whether she had really been living with me for such a reason, she stopped laughing and said in her normal quiet tone, "Can't you tell I'm joking? I'd intended to use my money to set up some business, but I didn't know what kind. Now several years later, I'm twenty-seven and still unmarried. After I started living with you and saw how you idled away each day, I realized we really needed to do something. So I wondered if there might be some business we could start with the money I've saved that would put enough food on the table, while being something you could get energetic about and sink your teeth into."

She hesitated but finally asked, "What are those scars on your neck and chest?" I was silent. My silence continued until she stood up and said, "Just as I thought. You won't tell me." She paid the bill, then waited for me by the door.

We got into the car, and when we turned onto the congested highway, I realized we were close to where I used to live. I had been taken in by my uncle in Ikuno Ward, who supported me through junior high school, high school, and then college. He died three years ago, and now my aged aunt lives there quietly with her son (who is three years older than me and works at a bank), his wife, and three grandchildren. My aunt was the most grief-stricken about our divorce. She who raised me, who treated me no differently from her own children, lived in the vicinity. I felt a lump in my throat. It has been more than two years now that I've been unable to repay the nearly 600,000 yen she secretly lent me when jobs at various companies didn't work out and after a number of my failed business attempts. During these two years, not only have I not visited her, but I have not even called. To my aunt, that 600,000 yen was an important part of her income for her old age; yet I took her generous loan and have not communicated with her since.

I mentioned to Reiko that I used to live in the area. It was the first time I had told her anything about my past. As I said this, I also recalled that a girl in my high school class had taken over her parents' beauty shop. If the request came from me, she might subscribe to our brochure. I hesitated, thinking that if I showed up, word of it might get back to my aunt, since the shop was only about a ten-minute walk from my aunt's house. But then I thought how I would like to be liberated from Reiko's insistence that we not go home until we got a contract, and I also wanted to please Reiko, who was working herself into a sweat bowing and scraping to beauty shop owners.

I drove past my old high school and parked the car along the main shopping street. From Reiko I took the folder of sample brochures, contract forms, and mock-ups, and began walking away, after saying an old friend managed a beauty shop nearby and I did-n't know whether she would sign up, but I would try to see her. A beauty shop is a difficult place for a man to enter, you know. When I peered inside, my old school friend, now quite matronly in appear-ance, was near the door, busily giving orders to her employees. I walked past her spacious shop several times but couldn't bring myself to go in, until finally I lost my nerve completely and decided to give up. Just when I was about to leave, someone called out, "Arima!" I turned around to see my friend looking at me as she held the glass door open and leaned out.

"So it *is* you! What were you doing walking back and forth in front of my shop?" she asked. I answered that I had a favor to ask, but found it difficult to go inside places like beauty shops. We hadn't met since our class reunion toward the end of the year you and I got married, but she said, almost nostalgically, that she rec-ognized me the instant she saw me. She invited me inside and asked me what the favor was. I sat down on the sofa in the waiting area and took out the sample brochures and mock-ups. Fearing I might lack credibility if I told her I just started recently, I lied and said that I had been doing this work for three years. She looked carefully at the sample brochures for a long time, then asked for reassurance that the rule of only one shop per area would be strictly observed.

I showed her the map: "Your area would go to about here, wouldn't it? If I make a contract with you, I will definitely not sign up any other shops in this area."

"So they're twenty yen apiece," she said to herself as she deliberated.

I pointed to the list of prices by the entrance and said, "Every beauty shop is trying to come up with special expertise and services for its customers. In addition, if your shop publishes a monthly brochure, your clientele will compare you to other shops and decide that you put more effort into service. It's giving back to customers a mere twenty yen of the five or six thousand they pay you. That's a bargain, isn't it? The name of your shop will appear in this box on the front page, along with the owner's name, so clients will read it without feeling that they've received something ready-made. That's why our company has the strict policy of only one shop per area. As many as a hundred and twenty shops in the Kansai region have already been subscribing for two years." I was so desperate that I didn't hesitate to resort to outright lies.

She asked, "How do you get the brochures to the shops every month? If you mail them, you'd need mailing costs over and above the four thousand yen, wouldn't you?"

Her question took me by surprise. If I said the mailing charge was included in the price, it would bring our profits down, but if I said clients paid the cost of mailing, the price would go up and she might not subscribe. It was a point Reiko and I had not discussed.

Without missing a beat, I answered that I would deliver the brochures by car at the end of each month, and that we had a system of taking them directly to shops and collecting the fee on delivery. In that case, she said, she would sign, and immediately filled in the form and set her seal on it, noting as she did so, "One set of two hundred copies won't be enough for us. We really need six hundred, but to begin with I'd like to try four hundred. If I feel they're not bringing any results, may I quit anytime?"

"Of course. But if you keep giving these to your customers, in time they'll be just like a billboard for your shop. That's why a hundred and twenty shops have continued for two years now."

Once our business was concluded, she had one of her employees bring some cold juice and began reminiscing about old times, talking on and on about how so-and-so in A class was now a detective at a police station in such-and-such a place, and how so-and-so in B class had got married and had a child but had died the following year of breast cancer. She wouldn't let me escape. I wanted to get back to Reiko and was feeling impatient. But her contract was for four hundred copies, after all—and would go up to six hundred if her customers liked them—so I couldn't very well rush off. I ended up talking to her for almost an hour.

By the time I walked through the street and returned to the

car, Reiko was waiting for me with a worried look on her face. Without saying a word, I held the contract in front of her face.

"Four hundred copies?" she stammered, and clutched the form to her chest.

"OK, now let me off the hook," I said as I drove the rattle-trap toward the main highway. Reiko's eyes were aglow, and she asked me over and over how I pulled it off. I told her everything, including what I had said and what the owner of the shop had asked.

"You really *are* great at this, aren't you? I'm inexperienced and can't think so fast."

Reiko was showing how impressed she was with me, but I reminded her that I did it just this once because I wanted to go home—"It's really no concern of mine."

Then she replied, as if it were a matter of course, "Yes, but you'll make the deliveries at the end of the month, won't you?"

Reiko apparently intended to mail the finished brochures to each beauty shop. She had inquired at the post office, and was informed it would cost three hundred yen to send two hundred copies. "I've told the shops I've gone to that there would be an additional mailing charge of three hundred yen. Potential customers really seem to feel the difference between four thousand yen and four thousand three hundred yen. Three hundred yen isn't much, but it must seem like a lot to someone who's paying. So, yes, it would be better to deliver them by car. Gasoline won't cost much, and it will make a better impression on the shops. You really are smart, aren't you?"

I had landed right into Reiko's palm. From that day on, I drove her around every day making sales. The day before the twenty thousand brochures were due to be printed—and the overprinting of the names and telephone numbers of each of the shops—Reiko had concluded seven more contracts, bringing the total to twenty-six. We were still in the red, but Reiko was as pleased as could be. Although there were only twenty-six shops, they were spread out between Kyoto and Kobe, and I didn't finish the deliveries until eight in the evening. Reiko treated me to beer and steak at a restaurant near our apartment. "Treated" is the right word—I felt like a child getting sweets as a reward. Reiko was in high spirits, and I returned to the apartment absolutely exhausted.

For three days, I did nothing but loaf around the apartment. On the evening of the fourth day, Reiko and I went to the public bath (our apartment is in an old building that lacks such amenities). After we bathed, we had a cold drink at a coffee shop, then returned home. A white car was parked in front of our apartment building; the young man in the driver's seat stared at me. When our eyes met, he nonchalantly looked away. His general appearance and the way he averted his eyes somehow bothered me.

Pretending not to notice, I opened the door to the building and went upstairs with a feeling of foreboding. Another man was standing in front of the door of our apartment. He was wearing a cap with red polka dots, and seemed a bit shady. Suddenly, I remembered something. When my previous business venture failed and we were facing bankruptcy, I did everything I could to settle matters so there would be no trouble afterward. But one promissory note I couldn't trace. It was for 986,000 yen and was due in three months. I tried to cancel it, but was unable to discover where it ended up. When I saw the man standing in front of our door, I realized the two must be related.

"Are you Mr. Arima?" he asked. When I answered in the affirmative, he said that he had something to talk to me about and wanted to come inside. He spoke in the manner typical of men like him. When I refused, saying that it was not my apartment but hers, and that if he wanted to talk, I would rather do it elsewhere, he said in a soft tone of voice, "We could talk here, but it would disturb the other tenants." Then, kicking the door with the tip of his shoe, he went on, "I've been waiting here in this heat for two hours. And, besides, I don't want to shout."

When I told Reiko to go somewhere for about an hour, he glared at me and, in an increasingly cutting tone, said that he wanted my wife to hear what he had to say. I knew only too well the methods used by money collectors like him, but I let him in. Taking off his cap, he sat down cross-legged on the tatami, took a piece of paper from the inside pocket of his black jacket, and placed it in front of me. It was the promissory note for 986,000 yen, bearing my registered seal.

"Before we go any further, I should tell you that this woman is not my wife and she has no connection with any of this."

"Oh really? But you live together, don't you?" he said, taking off his black jacket. Underneath he was wearing a purple shirt of some thin material, through which his skin was visible. It was unbuttoned down to the middle of his chest, which glistened with perspiration. His back was tattooed. He was a mere baby gangster and didn't strike me as much of an opponent. Yet, depending on the time and place, a baby gangster is sometimes more dangerous. Reiko turned pale at the sight of his tattoo.

"You remember this promissory note, don't you?" he asked, adding that he was working for a certain business, and when he went to collect from a client, he had been forced to accept payment in the form of this promissory note. "Of course, the reasonable thing would be for the client to pay, but unfortunately he died, leaving nothing of much value. Which means that the only thing we can do is get the money from 'Arima,' whose seal is on the note. It took us six months to find you." That's a line every collector uses, and it's useless to reason with people like him. I answered simply that I had no money.

"No money… You think you can get away with an excuse like this?" When I brushed him off, saying that he couldn't get blood from a stone, he responded threateningly, "Which do you value, your money or your life? And you know it wouldn't be just *your* life." Then he looked sharply at Reiko, who was sitting next to me. Reiko shuddered.

"You can just sue me, can't you?"

"If you get sent to prison, we wouldn't get a dime. I'm sure by now you've figured out what kind of man I am. There are five or six people at the bottom of the Yodo River who tried to go through the police or the courts."

I saw that Reiko was now visibly trembling, and I said, "Well, it can't be helped. You'll have to kill me." It was no mere bluff; I felt prepared to die. The blood drained from the man's face.

Reiko stood up and from a hiding place in the chest of drawers took out a paper bag containing a million yen, plus some interest, that she had received from the recently matured certificate of deposit. She placed it before the man. Before he was able to grab it, I snatched it away and placed it on Reiko's lap: "This is your money. You don't need to do this."

The man then stood up and said, "Well, you'll need some time to think about it. It doesn't matter who pays. Money is money. I'll stop by again tomorrow. And I'll take either the money or your life." With that parting shot, he left the apartment.

I told Reiko not to worry. "Tomorrow, I'll move out and won't come back. Even a guy like him can't very well take money from a woman I'm not married to. If he comes back tomorrow and threatens you, call the police immediately. There are two things these thugs are most afraid of: being stood up to and getting involved with the police. That's why they may talk big, but they won't resort to violence. Instead, they attack gradually and psychologically. They'll come by at four in the morning. Or they may barge in every day for an entire month and then suddenly disappear, waiting until their victims feel relieved and let down their guard. Then they'll come by again every day for days on end. Even if I'm not here, they may come and bother you for a while. But they won't lay a finger on you."

In spite of my reassurances, I felt apprehensive, all the more so because we were dealing with a baby gangster. Now that he knew Reiko had money, he might try to intimidate her even if I were no longer around. I was tired of always being on the run, but there was nothing I could do but move out. Reiko had never spent anything on herself, so how could she now throw away her money for someone like me—money that she had carefully saved over ten long years of standing at the cash register in the supermarket? This seemed like the right time for me to leave. You, then Yukako, and now Reiko. Every woman I get involved with ends up having an awful experience. Now I remember why I had this strange feeling of relief when I decided to divorce you. But it was all very different this time, and I felt an aching emptiness in my heart.

Reiko, in tears, said, "I'll pay the money. A million yen is nothing."

"Don't get involved in what's not your business. I don't care anymore what happens to me. Luck's just not on my side, and as long as you're with a man like me, you'll fail as well."

I spread out my futon, turned off the light, and lay down. I realized that what I had said to the collector reflected my true feelings: "You'll have to kill me." I recalled my tense yet utterly vacuous state of mind as I spoke the words. I was prepared to die. With my eyes shut, I mentally whispered those words again.

That night I dreamed of you. It was a short dream, but it has stayed fresh in my mind. Coming out of the woods at Dokko Pond, you made your way steadily up the mountain path. I followed at some distance but was unable to catch up with you. You waved to me, laughing and signaling for me to hurry. I was leading a little girl, who had features just like yours, by the hand. She was about four or five. It was just a short dream; nothing else happened.

Around ten o'clock the next morning, I stuffed my belongings into a bag and left the apartment. Reiko didn't try to stop me. She was sitting motionless at the kitchen table with her back to me and didn't turn around when I walked out. After leaving Reiko, I had no idea where I should go. I couldn't very well go to my aunt's place in Ikuno. I still hadn't returned the 600,000 yen she had lent me, and I wasn't so shameless as to show up now. I recalled an old friend from my high school years by the name of Ôkuma, who was still single and was a cancer researcher at a university medical school in Kyoto. One time he had put me up for about two weeks after I left a woman, and I had also hidden out once at his apartment to evade creditors. I called the university from a public phone and, after being connected to Ôkuma, I asked him if he could put me up for a while. He responded, "What? Have you been chased out by a woman again?" He told me to wait for him in front of Kyoto National Museum at six o'clock, then quickly hung up. Whenever we meet, he wants to go barhopping and won't allow me to get away, but on the phone he is always so abrupt I can't believe it's the same guy.

I decided to go to Umeda for a while. Happening upon a railroad crossing just as the barrier was being lowered, I stopped. The summer sun blazed down on me. As the train approached, I thought, "Ah, it's coming! It's getting closer and is about to pass in front of me at a ferocious speed." I don't know why I thought this, but the moment I did, my heart began to pound and I felt as if all the blood in my body had swooshed down to my feet. The train was almost at the crossing. I closed my eyes tightly and gritted my teeth. The train passed, the barrier went up, and cars and people began to move. I realized I was unconsciously clutching the bicycle rack of the person next to me. From the moment the train appeared until it rushed past, two forces seemed to be violently contending within me.

I hailed a cab and told the driver to take me to Umeda. It was chilly in the air-conditioned cab, but perspiration oozed all over my body and wouldn't stop. In the ten years since the incident with Yukako, even at times of the greatest despair and frustration, I had never wanted to die. But watching Reiko shudder when that baby gangster of a collector presented my promissory note while making blustering threats, I was no longer just disappointed or frustrated. I felt as if I were sinking into a deep, pitch-black hole. "I don't care if I die. What good will it do to go on living? Is it worth starting my life all over again if Reiko has to throw her hard-earned money into the gutter?" Such were my thoughts.

I boarded a train on the Hankyû Line out of Umeda and got off in Kyoto's Kawaramachi district. Striding through the crowd, I could see the department store where Yukako had worked. I went into a movie theater that was showing some violent foreign film about a naked beauty and an invincible spy alternately entwining their bodies and being chased by enemies. It was after four when I left the theater, still two hours to go before meeting Ôkuma. The National Museum was rather far, and as I could think of nothing else to do, I headed there at a leisurely pace. Though the sun had begun to take on a reddish cast as it descended, it was still hot, and I dropped into a coffee shop on the way. Leaning back against the chair with my eyes closed, I must have dozed off for a while. When I awoke and looked at my watch, far more than "a while" had passed: I had been sound asleep for nearly two hours. I hurriedly left the coffee shop.

Ôkuma was standing in the graveled area by the museum entrance. "I got here at five thirty. You've kept me waiting a whole hour."

We went into a small restaurant nearby, one where Ôkuma said he occasionally had a drink. "Today's payday, so it's on me. You don't have any money anyway, do you?" he said, ordering a large pitcher of beer and several fish dishes.

I had left the apartment wearing a jacket over my polo shirt, but had taken off the jacket in the cab and was carrying it. The proprietress of the restaurant offered to hang it up, and while handing it to her, I noticed an envelope stuffed into the inside pocket. I looked in the envelope and found ten 10,000-yen bills. Reiko must have surreptitiously put them there. I crammed the envelope into my back pocket.

With some alcohol in him, Ôkuma began his usual nonstop chatter. Sumo wrestler so-and-so was sure to reach the second-highest rank at the next tournament.... A pitcher from such-and-such high school would join a professional team next year, with a hundred million yen behind the scenes to promote him.... Then his rambling shifted to abstruse mathematical equations and chemical symbols—drawn on the countertop with a chopstick dipped in beer—and to different theories on cancer treatment from around the world. "Cancer, you see, is part of oneself," he said. When I asked him what he meant, he explained in a voice slurred with drink, "Cancer is not something that invades from outside, but something that originates within one's body. It's foreign matter, but it's not something apart from us. It's something you always have inside you that turns into toxin-emitting cells, which can reproduce. In order to kill cancer, the fastest way is just to die." He stroked his unshaven chin as he made these pronouncements— how serious he intended them to be was impossible for me to determine—then stood up and asked for the bill.

We went to three more bars. By the time we got to the last one, Ôkuma was so drunk that he couldn't walk straight. But I didn't feel the least bit tipsy. I glanced at my watch: nine o'clock. It occurred to me that the collector with tattoos all over his back would probably be showing up at Reiko's apartment about now— or not just showing up, but perhaps barging in and threatening Reiko—and I was worried. After some hesitation, I went to a pay phone at the end of the counter and dialed her number. Until recently, she didn't have her own telephone and had to be paged by the caretaker, but since starting the business she said a telephone was absolutely necessary and had a line connected about a week ago.

Reiko answered. As soon as she recognized my voice, before I could say anything, she begged me to come back. "The man returned at about eight o'clock. I paid the 986,000 yen, and he gave me your promissory note. It's all over now, so come back," she said, sobbing. When I told her that I was calling from Kyoto, she started crying even harder and shouted, "If you're not here, I can't continue the business, can I? The next brochure has to be compiled and sales have to be made. If you hadn't been here, I would never have wanted to start this business in the first place. It was because of you that I racked my poor brain and thought it up. With this business, I'll recover a million yen in no time. If you're determined to leave me, then do it after I've earned 986,000 yen. Otherwise, you're a thief!"

I thanked her for the cash. When I told her that I might use all the money she had put in the envelope before I came back, she said, "So use it up quickly. Use it up tonight and then come right back." Then there was only silence on the other end of the line; she seemed to be holding her breath waiting for my response. I told her that I would be there the next day just past noon and hung up. The suspicion suddenly nagged at me that, just maybe, Reiko had colluded with the collector in order to pin me down.

It became too bothersome to think anymore. I looked at Ôkuma, who was bent over with his face on the table, muttering something. I tapped him on the back and announced, "Hey, I'm off."

In a voice thick with drink, he roared, to no one in particular, "If you want to leave, then leave!"

I hailed a cab in front of the bar and told the driver to take me to the Kiyonana Inn in Arashiyama. Starting tomorrow, I'll once again be the slave of Reiko, I thought to myself. From this point of view, it all seemed so funny. I didn't yet feel like throwing myself heart and soul into Reiko's business, but I definitely had to do 986,000 yen's worth of work. But what a sly one Reiko was!

I recalled her face as she said, laughing, "I've been keeping you for a whole year for moments just like this." Though she said she was joking, it was no joke.

I couldn't suppress a chuckle, and the driver asked, "Did something good happen to you?"

I said, "I've been trapped by a woman. Completely trapped!"

The driver looked at me through the rear-view mirror and laughed. He replied, "Yeah, women are witches, aren't they?"

When I arrived at the Kiyonoya, I asked if the Bellflower Room on the second floor was available, explaining that I had stayed there before and had liked it very much. The clerk at the desk looked troubled as he asked, "Are you by yourself?" (They usually give this room to couples.) I said that I had once stayed there with a woman, but tonight I was by myself. If this was a problem I would gladly pay the same rate as a couple. The owner appeared, looked at me, and said, "You're welcome to stay wherever you like." Then he told the clerk to show me to the Bellflower Room. I remembered the owner, but he had apparently completely forgotten me.

When I entered the room, I was startled to see that not a single thing had changed in ten years. The landscape scroll hanging in the tokonoma alcove, the celadon incense burner in front of the scroll, the designs on the sliding panels—all were exactly the same as ten years ago. I looked at the face of the maid who brought the tea and was again surprised. It was Kinuko, the same woman who always used to bring tea to this room ten years before. She still uncannily looked as if she were in her forties. I was trying to hide my face as much as possible. I used to give her generous tips, and she would likely remember me.

"Would you like me to bring you something to eat?" she asked.

I said that I had already eaten and told her just to bring some beer.

"There's beer in the refrigerator. You can help yourself. You'll be billed when you check out."

The refrigerator was the only new item in the room. I handed two thousand-yen bills to the maid and asked her to bring breakfast at eight the next morning. She bowed and left without saying a word. I went into the bathroom near the entrance of the room, and began drawing a bath. Then I changed into the cotton bathrobe provided by the inn and waited for the tub to fill. The window facing the garden was open, and a cool breeze was blowing into the room, accompanied by the sound of rustling leaves. As I listened to the running water, it struck me: Yes, ten years ago I would look out this window, listening to the sound of water filling the bath while waiting for Yukako.

Yukako would enter the room by opening the sliding panels just inside the door, sometimes looking downcast, sometimes with a sparkle in her eye, sometimes looking dazed and pressing her hands against her flushed cheeks, sometimes drunk, and other times completely sober. I was overwhelmed by the illusion that any minute Yukako might really show up. Reiko's grandmother's words about meeting her sons again in this life came to mind with a palpable sense of reality. However, if I were to believe Reiko's grandmother, Yukako could never be reborn as a human being. Even so, I still had the impression that Yukako might enter the room any moment. When the bath was full, I climbed into it.

I heard the maid announce herself as she entered the room to lay out the futon. As she departed, she called out, "I've left some antimosquito coils for you." I washed myself and shampooed my hair very carefully. I spent an inordinate amount of time scrubbing my entire body, even lathering my toes one at a time. After I got out of the tub and was toweling myself dry, I caught sight of my torso in the mirror. The scars on my neck and chest now seemed merely like elongated welts, but when I stepped nearer to the mirror and looked closely, I could see the distinct marks of the stitches. I clearly recalled the slimy sensation of the blood running down my neck to my chest when Yukako slashed me, and I stood up on the bedding, confused.

Wearing my bathrobe, I sat on the sofa under the window that faced the garden and poured myself a glass of beer. Spread out in the middle of the room were a thick futon mattress for one person and a light summer coverlet. Smoke from the antimosquito coil rose above the bed in lazy curls. Puffing on a cigarette, I fingered the scar on my neck.

Ten years ago something was set in motion in this room in the Kiyonoya, and I felt I understood a little of what that "something" was. It wasn't just my splitting up with you or my steady descent as a human being; it was much greater. What was it that I saw as I was about to die? In a previous letter to you, I wrote that "it was my life itself." But what was "life itself"? Why did all the scenes from my past flash vividly through my mind, as if a film were being shown in reverse? What was the reason for this phenomenon?

I listened, just as I had done ten years before. I listened for the sound of Yukako's footsteps walking down the corridor toward this room. I passed several hours this way, smoking and drinking beer, caressed by the cool breeze. I glanced at my watch: it was after three o'clock. I turned off the light. It was too dark, so I turned on the small fluorescent light above the tokonoma alcove. On the edge of the alcove sat the green telephone that was connected to the front desk. Yukako had knocked it over as she was dying, and so saved my life.

What images from the past flashed through her mind as she was about to die? And what kind of life did she see her dying self changing into? I can't believe the strange experience I had was a chance phenomenon that happened only to me. I feel certain Yukako also drifted through the same state. When faced with death, don't all people see the acts they've committed? Don't we all inherit the anguish or the serenity formed from the way we've lived, and become just inextinguishable "life," blending into the time and space that is without beginning or end in the limitless universe?

In the darkness, staring at the tokonoma, which was bathed in a bluish light, I could see Yukako lying facedown, dead. Who could say for certain that it was wild fancy? Or who could prove that it was reality? But when we die, we'll understand. And there are surely many things hidden in our lives that will only become clear when we die.

Morning came without my having slept a wink. The cicadas started trilling at around six o'clock, and the summer sun filtering through the green leaves of the trees made them flicker in delicate hues. At eight o'clock the maid brought me breakfast. Looking at the undisturbed bedding, she turned to me with an inquiring expression and asked, "Didn't you sleep?" I answered that the cool breeze felt so good that I ended up falling asleep on the sofa. The maid put the futon back in the closet and began to set out my breakfast. After I washed my face and sat down at the table, she served me rice. Following an interval of silence, she mentioned that every year on that day she made sure to put some flowers in the tokonoma. She had recognized me after all.

"You haven't aged at all, have you, Kinuko?"

She smiled back. "You haven't either, Mr. Arima."

"No, I have changed."

Without responding to this, she explained that she had recognized me immediately the night before when she brought me tea, and that after many years of this work, she was usually able to tell what sort of people guests were by just looking at them. In the case of a couple, no matter how they might try to appear as if they were married, they never managed to fool her; she would get a general idea of their relationship, and she was rarely wrong. She sensed that the woman who died in this room was a hostess in a nightclub, a first-rate one, while her male partner worked for a respectable company and was likely a very capable man. Moreover, she could even tell that he wasn't single but had a family. Kinuko, who must be over fifty now, sat across from me as I ate my breakfast, and continued to talk quietly as she poured tea and refilled my rice bowl.

"I had taken the day off, and it was not until noon the next day when I came to work that I learned of the incident with you and the woman. Police officers were still coming in and out, and the owner was in a foul mood, saying that something unfortunate like this would be bad for business. I heard about what happened. Rather than being shocked, I was sad. She was such a beautiful person, like a flower bursting into bloom. Only some months later did I hear that the man didn't die. I haven't been able to forget the two of you. The woman who died was such a beauty that I was especially fascinated by her, and I could never forget her. That's why every year, when the day arrives, I buy some flowers without telling the owner, and arrange them in the tokonoma." Then she added, "She looked different every time," and fell silent.

When I finished breakfast, I asked her to call a cab for me. Though I had said I would pay the double rate for the room, when I received the bill, I was only charged for a single occupancy. I took the cab to the Hankyû Line station, and from there returned to Umeda, back to Reiko's apartment.

Tomorrow, I have to start compiling the next brochure. When this is done, I have to drive Reiko around to sell them. Oh yes, after ten years, she finally quit her job at the supermarket. It's always the same—just when I think she is being as submissive as a child to me, she gives me a swift slap on the rear and brilliantly succeeds in keeping my nose to the grindstone.

If I may digress, there is something I want to write to you

about, but I'll try to make it as concise as possible. You wrote, "Father is the sort of person who can see through other people." Indeed, it's frightening how accurately Hoshijima Terutaka can see into someone else's mind. I remember him with great fondness. He is a true workaholic, having created the Hoshijima Construction empire in his lifetime. Even at home he projected an inaccessible dignity and an unknowable detachment, and to his employees at the company he was a formidable boss. But I have one memory of him that is particularly unforgettable.

One day I was summoned to his office. I knocked on his door expecting another scolding. But he wasn't sitting in his chair— he was lying on the sofa, folding paper airplanes with a serious expression on his face and flying them around the room. Seeing me, he threw an airplane at me, then motioned for me to sit next to him. He whispered in a small voice, "There's something I'd like to talk to you about. Don't tell anyone, especially not Aki."

As I was wondering what it could possibly be, he gazed off into space and mumbled, "There's a woman I'm in love with. We're getting to be on intimate terms."

Surprised, I asked who she was. He mentioned a large Japanese-style restaurant in the Minami area of Osaka that he often patronized when entertaining for business purposes. I won't say which one.

I leaned forward and asked, "Is it a geisha? Or the owner?" Replying that it was neither, he sat up and glared at me, "Idiot! The owner is seventy-one years old!"

Then he mentioned the name of the woman, the youngest

daughter of the owner. Her husband had died two years previously, whereupon she had returned to her parents' house and now often appeared at the restaurant in her mother's stead. I had often met her myself. She was about thirty-two or thirty-three and looked striking in a kimono. I remember her as a beautiful, refined woman, with a nose that was thin but high-bridged, ample cheeks, and long, slanting eyes.

"By 'getting to be on intimate terms,' you mean you haven't done anything yet?"

My question elicited a glare from him, and he answered that it was just a matter of time. Then his expression suddenly turned pathetic, and he said, "I'm sixty and she's thirty-two. What should I do?"

I said, "She's a widow, and it has been seven years since you lost your wife. I don't think either of you has anything to feel ashamed of."

Puffing hard on his cigarette, he looked at me and muttered, "It's all very odd. Whether I'm working or meeting people, her face keeps popping up in front of me, and I can't relax."

I said with a laugh, "It's love, isn't it?"

He replied in a listless voice, "Could it be love?"

I asked how it started, but he wouldn't say. I couldn't believe the restaurant owner's daughter—a woman in her prime who had lost her husband two years earlier—would 'get to be on intimate terms' with Hoshijima Terutaka.

He said, "Hey, I trust you, so I'm asking you for advice. What do you think I ought to do?"

I answered with a broad grin, "It'll make you young again."

About three weeks later I was once again summoned to his office. This time he was waiting for me at his large executive desk, resting his chin on the palm of his hand.

I asked, "Is it about work? Or the other matter?"

He said, "The other matter. It pains me to talk about it. I ended up going to an inn with her. Actually, events made it more a matter of *having* to go to an inn with her. I was feeling a bit embarrassed, but she appeared to be prepared. I thought I'd still have no problem, yet there I was embracing a naked woman, and I couldn't get ready for action. The more impatient I got, the more hopeless it was. Do you understand how pathetic I felt then? I was really depressed."

Suppressing an urge to laugh, I tried to comfort and encourage him: "No doubt you were just nervous. Anyway, you were in love. It happens a lot. Next time, everything will be fine."

Looking up at me, he muttered dejectedly, "Yeah, I was really nervous." Then he resumed his usual company president countenance and reminded me that he had confided in me and that I was absolutely not to tell you. He never spoke to me about it again.

I don't know what happened to him and the woman. He didn't tell me any more than a fraction of what went on between them. No doubt he kept a lot of memories of her hidden in his heart, never sharing them with anyone. And this is just my hunch, but I bet he never attempted to do anything with her again. The look on your father's face when he muttered, "Yeah, I was really nervous," was like that of a little boy who had just made a terrible mess of something. For the first time, I felt a deep bond with Hoshi-jima Terutaka. Even now, I still harbor an image of him as a warm and tender person, who was also an excellent businessman. This is a story from the distant past that I had been absolutely forbidden to tell you.

Sincerely,
Yasuaki

September 18

Dear Yasuaki,

Early this afternoon I read your lengthy letter sitting at my table next to the window in the Mozart coffee shop. When I finished and returned home, Kiyotaka showed me his practice booklet for the hiragana syllabary, which he is now learning. He recently completed everything from a through *ma*, and today was writing words with the syllable *mi*. The ruled squares of the booklet were filled with the letters for *mizu*. Some were shaky or misshapen, while others slipped way outside the ruled squares, but they were perfectly legible. The next page was filled with the letters for *michi*.

After praising Kiyotaka for his progress, I wiped a speck of blue paint from the corner of his eye. Turning the page, he said, "There's one more." The letters for *mirai* were lined up. I asked why the teacher had made them write *mirai* even though they hadn't yet learned to write the syllable *ra*, but Kiyotaka said he didn't know. So I asked him how he was able to write *ra*, and he said the teacher just wrote *mirai* on the blackboard without saying anything, then had the students read *mirai* aloud several times. Even though they hadn't learned *ra*, he told them to copy *mirai* from the blackboard so they would know the word. Kiyotaka said that the teacher had told them *mirai* meant "tomorrow" and "the future."

In our correspondence, we've talked almost entirely about

165

the past, and when I compared our letters, I realized this is particularly true for me. Yet you are more caught up in the past than I. As if obsessed, you are trapped by everything that continues to emerge from the tragedy ten years ago. But what is the past? Lately, I've been seeing my "present" as definitely a product of my "past." Not a particularly momentous discovery, and actually just common sense, but since I had never really thought of my life in such a way, I felt I had made a great breakthrough. The past undoubtedly has the function of producing the present. But what about the future? Is the future unalterable by being already fixed by the past? Is there no way to change the future? Because of Kiyotaka, I can't help thinking that such an idea is ridiculous. When I look at him, I feel a surge of courage. At times I feel disheartened or disappointed, but then I reconsider, shake myself free, and feel ready to battle on again.

For some years, Kiyotaka wasn't even able to sit up, and he was five before he could say "Mommy" or "Daddy." I can't begin to tell you how much effort it took before he was able to button and unbutton his clothes. Now he's almost nine, and compared to a year ago he's a little quicker in getting around on his crutches. He can even say some tongue twisters correctly, although slowly, and he can articulate what he wants. And though I thought it would never be possible, he can do simple sums, albeit slowly. Someday, for sure, I'll show everyone how I've helped him become a normal person. It may take ten years, or even twenty. And there may be obstacles he'll be unable to surmount no matter what. But I'm determined to help Kiyotaka become as close to an ordinary person as possible, to raise him to be someone who can work responsibly on his own. Even if he can't do anything more than serve tea, that's fine. Even if he can't do anything more than pack finished products into cardboard boxes, that's fine. I'm determined to make him into someone who can work for a wage with dignity, even if it's a pittance.

Your letters have made me think hard. I, myself, gave birth to Kiyotaka—an all-too-obvious fact that has led me to a great discovery. I used to think being born with a burden of misfortune was Kiyotaka's problem, and that it must be his karma. His karma is surely involved, but there's more to it than this. One day, I suddenly received something like a divine revelation: it wasn't anyone's fault. My own karma required me to become the mother of a child like Kiyotaka. I had misunderstood things. There was a time when I gave in to feelings of resentment and convinced myself everything was your fault. I was unfair to take it all out on you. But it wasn't really anyone's fault. Kiyotaka's congenital disorder is a result of my karma. And you could say, too, it's Katsunuma Sôichirô's karma. But, having come to this realization, I wonder how I can overcome my karma. Must I just walk into the future passively, accepting whatever happens? No. I must live in the present and strive earnestly and ardently to make Kiyotaka as much of an ordinary person as possible. As his mother, I simply cannot sink into a state of resignation and nihilism. Just you watch—I'll make sure he will hold a job in the outside world!

I've ended up talking about Kiyotaka, and writing what sounds very much like a sermon. But please don't take it this way.

I just feel you're too trapped in the past and have forgotten the present. Some words Father once said come back to me: "People change. We're strange creatures that go on changing minute by minute and hour by hour." He was right. The way you live your life in the present will significantly alter the future you. The past is all water under the bridge and nothing can be done about it, but it also lives on, implacably creating the you of today. Yet I can't help feeling both you and I were oblivious to the fact that between the past and the future is a "present."

Please forgive me for the sermon, and don't tear up my letter in anger. I'm worried about you. Reiko's words, as you wrote in one of your letters, make me unbearably anxious: "I have this feeling that you're going to die." Surely she knows what kind of person you are. Even if you don't say anything, she must see right through you. Oh, please don't entertain thoughts of dying. Just to imagine such a thing breaks my heart. Why on earth did you go to Arashiyama and stay in that room?! Isn't this the sort of sentimentalism more suited to a twenty year old? And you had the nerve to quote the maid saying what a beauty Seo Yukako was!

Leaving everything else aside, I think Reiko's business is sure to succeed. You know, don't you, that my hunches are usually right? It's an interesting idea, one not many would think of. To be sure, 986,000 yen has been stolen from her savings—money important both for the business and for your lives—but Reiko valued you more than the money, and so she handed it over to the thug ungrudgingly. I strongly support your supporting her business. I have a feeling you'll find a hundred and fifty customers in no time.

Even if building up a clientele takes time, I'm convinced that one day you'll be serving a hundred and fifty shops. How long do you think it took Kiyotaka to put his thoughts and desires into words? Take one step at a time, the way Kiyotaka did. Even if my prediction is wrong, if you persevere you'll find at least one shop a week that will subscribe. That's four shops per month, forty-eight shops a year, and in three years you will have reached your goal. Only three years!

You'll probably be hard-pressed for money along the way. And there may be unexpected obstacles. But I think Reiko is a very strong person whose reticence and gentle exterior conceal the true grit of an Osaka woman. I have no doubt she's this kind of person—far stronger and more persevering than you. Moreover, she loves you passionately. I know. Precisely because of who I am, I know. Every time you're at your wit's end, about to give up on a business you've started, Reiko will no doubt come to your aid. She's the kind of woman whose latent strength reveals itself most apparently at such times. I'll be praying for you. I don't have any particular faith, so I don't know who to pray to. But I'll pray. Yes, I'll pray to the universe. I'll pray to the boundless, eternal universe for the success of your business and your future happiness.

Please write back. I'll be waiting for your letter, so please write.

Yours sincerely,
Aki

P.S. I almost forgot to mention this, but at the beginning of your letter you wrote that I was an attractive wife, and that even the "willfulness that came from my pampered upbringing was, in its own way, part of my charm. " As I read these words, I felt my face flush in spite of myself. But when you had an "attractive" wife, why did you continue a relationship with another woman for an entire year? I don't find your line about men being naturally promiscuous persuasive at all; and I cannot just reply, "Oh really?" And you mentioned that you "can't claim to know what things were like" with my new husband. But I know him better than anyone. I wasn't a good wife to Katsunuma Sôichirô. I was simply unable to love him as a husband. And then the brief dream you mentioned—it seems so pitiful. And the story—earthshaking for me—about Father's romance. I'm amazed how you male animals can be beguiled by a beautiful woman, no matter how old you are. Yet while I was reading your story, I caught myself snickering. I'm grateful you shared this as I thought you probably harbored some resentment toward Father.

October 3

Dear Aki,

Past, present, future... I accepted your sermonizing as being absolutely heartfelt, from the heart and soul of a mother who has raised a handicapped child, a mother who will yet be obligated to cope with many difficulties. And indeed, though I'm about to turn thirty-eight, I am amazed at my own immaturity. What you said is all too true. Why on earth did I return to that room in Kiyonoya? My ten years of decline—ending up like a broken shoe discarded in the gutter—are due solely to the fact that I am such a failure.

Nevertheless, I'm working now, trudging all around Osaka. At nine in the morning I stuff brochure samples, mock-ups, and contract forms into a briefcase and set out for the station with Reiko, who is similarly equipped. There we part, taking trains to areas on our day's schedule. Reiko is in charge of Osaka proper, while I attend to outlying cities such as Hirakata, Neyagawa, and Sakai. Since parking is now prohibited on most streets, if we made the rounds by car, we'd probably end up with parking tickets while talking to shop owners. Besides, the shops are often located on streets crowded with other shops, or in congested areas in front of stations, or in narrow lanes inaccessible to cars, and so we concluded it was best to go out on foot.

With a map in one hand, I look for beauty shop signs, and when I find one I first study its exterior. If the windows are dirty—or if there is no obvious effort put into attracting customers—then the owner will not be interested in a brochure, no matter how large the shop is. On the other hand, a small shop whose owner barely has time to do everything herself may have pictures of models with the latest hair styles or a sign saying "10% discount on weekdays," and even if she finds it a nuisance at first, she may eventually yield to my enthusiastic pitch and sign up for a month's trial.

Days spent visiting up to twenty shops and not getting a single contract make for very sore feet! In a tiny shop on the run-down outskirts of a town, I was surprised when the corpulent proprietress suddenly became indignant while listening to my explanation. Indirectly, she let me know what she was expecting: that I was supposed to address her as "madam." I was at a loss trying to understand why the owner of a two-bit beauty shop must be addressed as "madam," but she told me that it is customary in her business. Then she roundly dressed me down and turned me away, saying, "It's a waste of money to give each customer a scrap of paper for twenty yen." Now, no matter what kind of shop I go into—even if the person I address is obviously only an employee—I make it a point to ask: "Are you the madam?"

There have been occasions when, after I've persisted for nearly an hour, and the manager is on the verge of signing a contract, a young trainee will interrupt: "Madam, our customers wouldn't appreciate that sort of thing. You'd better refuse." And the deal is off. But then there was a day when I went to three shops in the morning, and all of them signed contracts without a moment's hesitation. After three weeks of walking around, I ruined my pair of good leather shoes, putting holes in both soles near the big toe and wearing the heels down. Shoes I had bought just for our sales trips looked like that after three weeks! On the other hand, my legs, which used to be weak, have become as sturdy as a mountain climber's. Reiko has already signed contracts with twelve shops, and I with sixteen. Combined with last month's twenty-six, we have fifty-four. In addition, we received twelve contracts from the five hundred direct mailings we sent out in one area, making for a grand total of sixty-six.

I might be exaggerating, but sometimes I feel this walking around looking for beauty shops is the essence of life itself. I've experienced standing at an intersection, pondering which way to go. I turn right, and as I walk the traffic thins out and I find I've wandered into an industrial zone where it would be unlikely to find a beauty shop, but I've gone so far I can't very well turn back. Nothing to do but keep on walking like an idiot down the factory-lined street, and by the time I finally reach an area that looks more residential, the sun has already set. What's worse is I have no idea where I am or how to get back, and I have a strong urge to just sit down on the spot. I wander home exhausted, not having set foot in a single beauty shop. Other times I reach an intersection, decide to start walking in a particular direction, and immediately happen upon a street with new homes and a new beauty shop where I easily seal a contract. As I walk every day, I strangely relish how my decision to turn right or left becomes the essence of life.

To deliver the brochures to the sixty-six shops, we have to use the car. Last month we were able to finish in one day, but this month it took three days. When the deliveries were done, we were able to take three days off. I went to a bookstore to purchase some books with useful material for the next brochure, and returned home to find Reiko sitting at the kitchen table. Her head was bowed and she had a grave look on her face. Though I asked what was wrong, she wouldn't answer. But when I sprawled out in front of the television set, she was unable to contain herself any longer and asked, "Who is Katsunuma Aki?"

I looked at Reiko, startled. I had put all your letters in the bottom drawer of my desk. Reiko used to be at the supermarket while I was loafing around the apartment, so I was able to collect your letters from the mailbox without her noticing. But two months ago, after Reiko was working for her own business full time, I asked the woman caretaker to take mail addressed to me out of the mailbox and give it to me later. For her help I gave her a 5,000-yen note, which she accepted with a smile. So I was mystified how Reiko could have known about you.

When I made no reply, Reiko took the bundle of your letters out of the drawer of my desk and placed it in front of me. She pressed me for an answer: "These seven letters—I can tell from the postmarks that the first one was sent on January 19. They're all incredibly thick, and they've just kept coming. Who is this 'Katsunuma Aki'?" The envelopes were all opened, and if Reiko had wanted to read the letters, she could have. But from her demand I knew she hadn't done so. She had resisted the urge to read them and waited for my return.

Then she said, "The first one is from 'Hoshijima Aki,' and the rest she addressed as 'Katsunuma Aki.' I want you to tell me who on earth she is."

I laughed: "Are you jealous?"

Keeping her head bowed, Reiko looked up at me: "No, I'm not."

"They're open. Why didn't you just read them on the sly?"

With her head lowered, Reiko muttered, "I wouldn't just read someone else's mail."

I had never told her anything about our past. Only once, I remembered, when we driving around selling, I mentioned that I used to live in Ikuno. Looking at the postmarks on your letters and putting them in order, I said to Reiko, "Feel free to read them." I apologize for letting someone else read your letters without your permission. I thought, though, that if she read some of them, she would understand everything without my having to say a word.

Anyway, they are long letters, and there are seven of them. Reiko moved to the table and began to read, while I watched television. I wanted her to fix something for dinner, but she kept on reading, as if devouring the letters. I asked if it was alright for me to go out and get a bite to eat, to which she gave a slight grunt without looking up.

I had dinner at a small restaurant nearby, then went to a coffee shop in front of the station. After about half an hour of sipping coffee, I didn't know what to do with myself. So I borrowed a memo pad and a ballpoint pen from the shop and, thinking about what sales techniques we would need to increase our clientele to a hundred and fifty shops—and what articles I ought to include in next month's brochure—I jotted down our present deficit along with our remaining savings. I was looking at the lines of numbers on the memo pad, my head resting on my hand, when I realized it had been a long time since I had been to a barber. Thinking I should go for a haircut the next day, it suddenly hit me: How about an advertising brochure for barbershops using the same method? The system would be the same, but the content would change to appeal to men. Yes, we should cast our net wider, to include barbershops as well. But there's no rush—only after the business with beauty shops is on track and is putting food on the table.

Leaving the coffee shop, I walked past the apartment and turned down the lane toward the printer. The glass door bearing the words "Tanaka Printing" was shut and the curtains were drawn, but a light was on in the work area, and I could hear a machine running. I opened the door to find the owner wearing smudged gloves and inspecting an inked printing plate. When I asked if he was still working, the man—who was slightly built, with salt-and-pepper hair and small eyes that were constantly blinking—stopped what he was doing and said with a friendly smile, "Come right in!" Cans of variously colored ink and sheets of paper used for test printings were scattered everywhere, leaving hardly enough room to walk. The whole place smelled of ink and paper. In wooden pigeon holes built into the wall were thousands of pieces of lead type glinting in the light cast by the fluorescent lamp. The owner brought out a chair for me to sit on. As he was taking off his gloves, he said, "You have forty more shops this month, don't you? At this rate, you'll be at a hundred and fifty in no time." When I answered that we were grateful for his careful work, he said in a manner without any hint of flattery, "I think your business will grow to five hundred shops." Then he continued, looking completely serious, "With five hundred shops, you would need one hundred thousand copies. But for some shops, two hundred copies won't be enough, and they'll want four hundred or even six hundred. If you go over one hundred thousand copies, I could bring my price of seven yen per copy down to five yen. A small shop like mine doesn't get many customers who pay 500,000 yen in cash each month, so hurry up and expand your business."

I mentioned the plan that had just occurred to me of including barbershops. Slapping his knee, he said, "That's a great idea! You can't just have beauty shops and not barbershops. Maybe you'll find more barbershops interested than beauty shops. Barbershops have been springing up like weeds these days, and if they do business the way they always have, they won't succeed. By all means try it! I didn't expect to make a profit myself at first. Maybe you could let me think of ways to adjust to your rate of growth."

He folded his arms and, looking at the ceiling, muttered his calculations. Five hundred barbershops… five hundred beauty shops… a thousand altogether… two hundred thousand copies… He went up the stairs at the back of the shop, brought down a bottle of beer and two glasses, and poured me a glass. Drinking the beer, we spent nearly an hour deep in conversation. He seemed to want to talk more, but I was anxious to tell Reiko about my plan, so I thanked him and extricated myself, and headed back to the apartment.

"A thousand shops?" I thought to myself as I walked. "Let's proceed slowly and carefully. I'm determined to reach a thousand within ten years." As I thought about ten long years, I felt like a baseball pitcher with only one pitch left, which would determine victory or defeat.

Reiko had moved away from the table and was leaning against the wall in a corner of the room, still absorbed in your letters. I stole a glance at her and saw that she had read almost to the end of your fourth letter. When I asked if she intended to read them all at once, and if she was going to have some dinner, she just grunted without looking up. I spread out my futon, changed into my pajamas, lay down, and turned on the television again. Reiko read the sixth and seventh letters lying next to me. It was after midnight when she finished. After returning the bundle of letters to the desk drawer, she turned off the light. She then switched on the kitchen light, took what looked like leftovers out of the refrigerator, and began to eat.

I turned off the television, got up to sit on a chair next to her, and lit a cigarette. She was crying, while eating chilled tofu, biting into slices of ham spread with mayonnaise, and stuffing her mouth with rice. She sniffled and wiped away tears with the back of her hand. No matter how much she wiped, the tears kept filling her big round eyes, flowing down her cheeks, and dropping onto the table. When she finished eating, she washed the dishes, still crying. Then she washed her face, brushed her teeth, and spread out her futon. She lay there without saying a word, the covers pulled up over her head.

For a while I sat alone at the kitchen table looking at Reiko. She was motionless under the quilt. Then I quietly approached her and slowly pulled the quilt back from her face. Her eyes were open, but she was still crying. I asked why she was crying so much. She looked at me with swollen eyes and stretched out her hands. After inviting me into her futon, she touched the scar on my neck. Reiko had only read the seven letters you sent and knew nothing of what was in the five I sent you. But, holding me tightly, she said, "I really like the person who was your wife." She didn't say anything else, no matter what I asked.

I crawled out of her futon, once again took out your letters from the desk drawer, and lined them up on the kitchen table. Without a word, I looked at the seven letters as I smoked a cigarette. You wrote once, didn't you, that you realized a time would come when we would have to end this correspondence? I glanced at Reiko, still covered by the quilt, unable to tell whether she had fallen asleep or was still sobbing, and I realized the time had come.

This will no doubt be the last letter from me. After I post it, my next destination will be to trudge down every street in Neyagawa City in search of beauty shops. And perhaps several years from now I'll get off at Kôroen Station on the Hanshin Line, walk through the familiar residential area, and come to your house, right next to the tennis club. Maybe I'll look up at your house, at the big old mimosa tree, and quietly go home. Please keep well. I'll be praying fervently that your son grows up just as you wish.

Sincerely,
Yasuaki

November 18

Dear Yasuaki,

I read your final letter sitting on a bench in the wisteria bower at the tennis club, basking in the warm, gentle autumn sun. It was as if I could see you before me, trudging around those neighborhoods, map in hand.

After I finished, I thought that I, too, should write a final message; yet days passed without my having any idea of what I should write. October came and went, and it was well into November, but for some reason I didn't feel like taking up my pen.

Then, on a Thursday with clear skies, Father took a day off for the first time in a long while. Around noon, as he was sitting on the verandah looking at the trees in the garden, he suggested that we visit Mother's grave. It was neither the autumn equinox nor the anniversary of her death—when such a visit would be customary—but I wanted to go. I asked Ikuko to pick up Kiyotaka when his school bus arrived in front of the station at three thirty, and I quickly got dressed. Father called his office and had them send a car. Then he put on a dark, olive-green suit he had made to order but never once wore because he thought it was too showy. He asked me, "How does this look?" It was very becoming.

While waiting for the car to arrive, we ate a light lunch. He said that after visiting the grave he would treat me to some fine

Kyoto cuisine, and that, considering the typically small portions of such fare, I should eat some lunch now.

You once went to Mother's grave with us, didn't you? I believe it was less than a month after we were married. When the Buddhist ceremony for the seventh anniversary of Mother's death ended, the three of us visited her graveyard under the trees at Yamashina, her birthplace.

When we heard the chauffeur, Mr. Kosakai, call to us, Father and I went out and got in the car.

"Take us to Yamashina. We're going to visit my wife's grave."

Mr. Kosakai has been Father's chauffeur for fifteen years. His oldest daughter just got married around the beginning of October. I had heard that his second daughter's wedding was set for this January, so I said, "Your daughter's wedding is soon, isn't it?"

"Our family is almost broke paying for these weddings," he replied.

I asked him why they were having another wedding so soon after the first, and Father laughed and answered for him: "If they don't have the wedding quick, the baby will be born first." Mr. Kosakai smiled sheepishly and said that his second daughter was already seven months pregnant, and if the baby was early, it might come before the wedding on January tenth, so they were very worried.

We left the Meishin Expressway and entered Kyoto, taking the highway to Yamashina. I noticed a florist's and asked Mr. Kosakai to stop, but Father said that no flowers were needed. It only made him sad to see wilted flowers in front of a grave. "I don't like the practice of offering flowers or ritual cakes." As the car moved off again, he muttered, "It's better not to decorate graves. The names of the dead people are carved on them, which is enough." Eventually we reached an area of rice paddies and passed a mountain village with farmhouses lining the road. The winding road was almost enshrouded in the thick stands of trees. "The autumn leaves are at their best now," said Father.

The graveyard, if you recall, is on the slope of a low mountain. The multicolored leaves of countless trees were fluttering in the wind as if to conceal the lonely place. At the entrance to the graveyard was a hut in which an old man was sitting. The hut was so small, it would barely offer one person protection from the rain or sun, and the inside was heady with the scent of incense. Candles, incense, and buckets and ladles were displayed. Father bought some incense from the old man and, after borrowing a bucket and a ladle and fetching water, we ascended the gentle slope toward the grave. Mr. Kosakai also got out of the car and followed us, saying that he, too, would like to pay his respects. Mother's grave is in the highest section. It is small, inscribed only with: "Hoshijima Fumi. Died December 14, 1963."

A lot of leaves had accumulated around the grave, so I walked back down to the old man to borrow a bamboo broom and dustpan. When I returned and started to sweep, Father stopped me, saying it was fine just the way it was. "No matter how much you sweep, more leaves will fall. There's no end to it. Her grave is exposed to the wind and rain, gets buried under fallen leaves, and will eventually be covered with moss. But that's alright, isn't it?" Then he stared at Mother's grave without even pouring some water from the bucket onto the stone, as is the custom.

"Well, at least let's light the incense," I said, borrowing his lighter.

"Just burn three sticks. If a lot of incense seeps into our clothes, we'll stink," he said, almost angrily.

I did as he asked. It occurred to me that had Mother been alive, she would surely have objected to our divorce in spite of the incident. She died when I was seventeen years old and of course knew nothing about you, but as I stared at her leaf-covered grave, I had the feeling she would have opposed our divorce. But all the "ifs" can't change anything. Speaking of things that can't be changed only amounts to idle complaining. Of the things I've lost during these thirty-five years, what were especially precious to me were you and Mother. But as I looked at her grave—and as I recalled your final letter—I felt that I had lost much, much more. Father, Mr. Kosakai, and I stood there for nearly twenty minutes in silence.

After the last of the thick smoke from the incense had vanished, Father said, "Shall we go?"

When we returned to the car, Father told Mr. Kosakai, "Take the other road." Rather than returning the way we had come, we went farther along the narrow, winding road. The stands of trees became thicker, and just as I was wondering where on earth we were headed, we came to the imposing gate of a restaurant named Shinoda. The middle-aged attendant, who recognized Father immediately, showed us to a room in the annex. The furnishings, the building materials, the layout offering a view of the garden from every room—all of this suggested much time and money had been put into the restaurant. Father invited Mr. Kosakai to join us, but, perhaps feeling awkward, he declined, saying that he had eaten lunch and was still full, and that he would wait in the car and listen to the radio.

The garden alone must have been about four thousand square meters. While simple in design, it was nevertheless splendid, achieving a marvelous harmony between the large, well-tended trees and the huge rocks with their thick covering of moss. A kimono-clad woman about my age or slightly older greeted us. Father introduced her to me as the owner, and after introducing me to her as his daughter, he asked her to bring what he usually ordered. With a sharp look, I asked if he used this place as a hideout. He explained that he had been entertaining clients here for about five years. He didn't know the owner's name, but said she had an extremely wealthy patron. Dishes of Kyoto cuisine were brought in, and while the owner made tactful conversation as she arranged them on the table, I turned my attention to the garden, gazing at a section a little to one side, where an abundance of scarlet leaves fluttered in the wind.

When the owner left, Father asked me what I thought of her. I replied that everything about her—her kimono, her obi— was striking, and that she was very beautiful. Father said she was an uncommon beauty—wealthy, intelligent, and a hard worker— but didn't have a pleasant voice. When I retorted that one's voice didn't make any difference, Father said with an earnest expression, "The voice is important. It reveals a person's true character. A good physician can tell the state of a patient's health just by subtle changes in her voice." Then a smile lit up his face as he moved his chopsticks toward the food in the lacquered vessels, and said, "Her voice lacks refinement."

Some time after we had finished our dessert of fresh fruit, Father pointed beyond the garden and said, "Some stone steps over there lead to a small shrine where the view of the autumn leaves is most beautiful." As he was putting on the garden sandals provided by the restaurant, he ordered, "You come, too, Aki." I sensed that he wanted to talk about something, and so I followed him. As he said, behind a large pine tree was a long path of stone steps, so narrow that we couldn't climb them side by side.

By the time we reached the top, I was out of breath. I spread out my handkerchief on a stone step and sat down behind Father. Looking at his back, I asked, "Isn't it about time you worked less?"

He replied, "At my age, I've finally managed to understand what work is. I've come to the opinion that working is living. I'll do a lot more work yet."

Looking out over the expanse of autumn leaves, he was silent for a while, then said, "I heard from Ikuko that you've been getting a lot of letters the past year, each one bearing the name of a different woman, and each one absurdly thick. About a month ago I was leaving for the office around noon. When my car pulled up and I stepped out of the house, there was a letter in the mailbox. I took it out. It was addressed to you, and the sender's name was 'Hamazaki Michiko.' I handed it to Ikuko and got in the car." Having said that much, Father turned to face me and added: "The handwriting brought back fond memories." We looked at each other in silence for some time. Finally he asked, "How is Arima doing?"

I decided to tell him everything, but I had no idea where to begin. I described in a haphazard and disorganized way about accidentally running into you on Mount Zaô a year ago, about our correspondence since then, about the circumstances of the incident, about Yukako, about your present business, and so forth. As I spoke, my voice began to tremble and tears welled up in my eyes.

"Relax," Father said gently.

When I finished, for some reason my heart was pounding and I was quite agitated. Father was silent for a long time. Then, with his eyes cast down, he asked, "Does Katsunuma hand over his university salary to you?" After I answered yes, Father seemed to ponder something, and then spat out, "That guy is worthless."

Father said he had Katsunuma investigated and found he was keeping a woman in Kobe. "You've probably known about it for a long time. He has a little girl by her who turned three this year. He must be doing extra work somewhere to get money for them," he said, lighting a cigarette. Then he asked, "Do you dislike Katsunuma? Do you think you could ever learn to love him?" Without waiting for my reply, he said angrily, "If you want to leave him, leave him. You're free to do so. You don't have to spend the rest of your life with a man you dislike. He's someone I pushed onto you. I didn't judge his character well. I've gotten you into one mess after another." He fell silent.

Controlling the tremor in my voice, I managed to blurt out, "I was the one who made Katsunuma the way he is. He's the one who got into a mess by marrying me. Somehow I was never able to love him."

I became quiet for a long time. Father did as well, and he stared at the autumn leaves without moving. I thought about Katsunuma. In my letters to you, I tried to avoid mentioning him. This in itself indicates how I feel about him. But he isn't a bad person. As Kiyotaka's father, he has felt no less grief and love for the boy than I, though he doesn't express it. He reads difficult books on Asian history, and is sincerely devoted to his research and his students at the university. Countless times I've seen him out on our lawn, patiently throwing a baseball to Kiyotaka to help him get stronger. After this he'd always sit cross-legged on the living room carpet, place Kiyotaka on his lap, and have long father-to-son talks. Why couldn't I come to love a man like him? And what did he feel when he looked at me? I suddenly thought about how things would be after Father passes away. He'll soon be seventy-one, and I don't know whether or not he'll be around to see Kiyotaka reach twenty.

Father had his back to me, and as I looked at his olive-green suit, I pictured Katsunuma's face during his talks with Kiyotaka. I felt an oppressive lump in my throat. The two overlapping shadows of Katsunuma and his student by the gate of the large mansion at dusk—no substance, just shadows—flitted darkly across my mind. It was then, for the first time, I felt something akin to affection for Katsunuma.

I stood up and looked at the somber trees around us. As I watched the leaves dancing merrily in the sunlight in hundreds of shades of red, yellow, green, and brown, I told Father that I wanted to leave Katsunuma. "I'll let him be the husband of that woman and the father of that three-year-old girl in the eyes of the world. I won't marry again. I'll do everything I can to help Kiyotaka grow up. Dad, please help me."

Father smoked another cigarette and stamped it out on the ground. He looked up and smiled at me as I stood there. "OK," he said as he got to his feet, and we made our way down the long, mossy stone stairway.

Before writing this letter, I reread everything I received from you. Various things occurred to me, all of them mental interweavings that are uniquely mine and impossible to put into words. I'll try, anyway, to convey what I mean. You said, didn't you, that seeing your own life made you afraid of living? But don't you see that experience could be the strongest encouragement for you to live the rest of your life? As I hold my pen, I am at a loss how to conclude this final letter to you. I wonder why those words came to me when I listened to Mozart's music: "Perhaps living and dying are the same thing." The words literally appeared out of nowhere. However, putting them down in a letter became a catalyst for you to tell me many things I didn't know. But they were words very unlike me to utter. And those words about the strange workings of the universe and of life, which the owner of the coffee shop mistakenly thought he heard me say, now fill me with something akin to profound fear.

Yukako, who plunged a knife into her neck and died. You, who watched yourself die but revived. My lonely father, who has grown old but is more devoted to his work than ever. Katsunuma

Sôichirô, who, with a secret family, no doubt worries about his three-year-old daughter. Kiyotaka and I, who, at the moment you were watching the mouse being eaten by the cat, were sitting on a bench in the dahlia garden gazing at the infinite expanse of stars. What inscrutable workings are woven into our lives!

I could write on endlessly, but the time has come for me to close this letter. To this universe—the universe that hides such strange workings—I pray for the future happiness of you and Reiko. After I put this letter in an envelope, address it, and put a stamp on it, I plan to listen to Mozart's Thirty-ninth Symphony for the first time in many months .

Goodbye, and please take care of yourself. Goodbye.

Yours Sincerely,
Aki

With his portrayals of ordinary people and his deceptively simple style, Teru Miyamoto (b. 1947) has built a considerable following among the reading public of Japan, an audience that is sure to be mirrored in the West as his works are translated. In his fiction, one rarely finds either traditional settings replete with cherry blossoms and kimonos, or the youth cult of J-pop and anime that informs the current image of Japan abroad; rather, one encounters in his work the everyday Japan of the vast majority of its people, gaining a clearer picture of their shared values than is projected in much other contemporary fiction.

Miyamoto's meteoric rise to literary acclaim over the past two decades began without special sponsorship or patronage. Only a generation ago, a novelist's career rarely commenced in Japan without the mentorship of an "establishment" (bundan) author, a practice which has largely succumbed to the promotional strategies of publishers and the demands of the reading public. A result of such a debut—which is typical of most new writers—is that, unlike such familiar "canonical" forebears as Sôseki Natsume (1867–1916) or Jun'ichirô Tanizaki (1886–1965), Miyamoto's oeuvre resists contextualization in terms of specific coteries, artistic pedigrees, or even influence from other authors, save the occasional similarity of his tone to that of Osamu Dazai (1909–1948) owing to coincidence rather than direct tutelage. By inclination rather than imitation, his works share with Tanizaki's later writing a distinct regional flavor—some in fact even appearing partly or entirely in Osaka dialect. His unusually large and devoted readership is, nevertheless, very diverse in background, and is amply represented in every part of Japan.

While Miyamoto's writing breaks free from the confessional "I-novel" strain that had dogged so much of prewar fiction in Japan, his novels and short stories do contain vignettes drawn from events in his own life. From his expulsion from kindergarten to his repeated failures at college entrance examinations, his early years would hardly seem to augur a successful literary career, which in his case began in earnest only after his marriage, the birth of his eldest son, and repeated bouts of tuberculosis that necessitate lengthy convalescences. His fiction achieves a rare blend of earthiness and reflective introspection. Philosophical musings are triggered by mundane events and given voice through characters that Japan's surge of economic growth in the closing decades of the past century have left behind. His 1982 novel, *Kinshu: Autumn Brocade,* fuses together numerous themes and motifs that appear perennially in his books. Consisting entirely of an exchange of letters between a divorced and long-estranged couple, this novel explores human relations from a perspective that is rarely examined.

Epistolary novels, once commonplace, have become a rarity in an age habituated to instant telecommunications, and alien to lengthy letters. Such an exchange between two characters, however, allows the exploration of their psyches through first-person narration, making possible fuller and more thoughtful articulation than would be the case through recorded conversations. This narrative strategy is well suited to the themes Miyamoto probes, and is particularly rewarding to readers who enjoy letters of prodigious length.

The mystifying relationship between life and death is the most salient theme that recurs throughout Miyamoto's works. In an interview, he once opined, "When all is said and done, the ultimate theme of literature is life and death." Nowhere is this theme presented more compellingly than in *Kinshu*, where the forces of life and death are represented in the music of Mozart. This will not appear unusual to readers familiar with the views of the Austrian composer, who wrote to his father in a letter dated April 4, 1787, that death, which is the "true ultimate goal of life," is our "true best friend," and "the key to our true happiness." The dean of modern Japanese criticism, Hideo Kobayashi, interprets this to mean that "death speaks from another world, from which it illuminates life." Miyamoto's essays give ample evidence of his familiarity with Kobayashi's writings on Mozart, and *Kinshu* expands on Kobayashi's ideas by suggesting that the pivot between life and death is karma, which each individual must learn to confront in order to achieve closure.

Another perennial theme in Miyamoto's fiction, which appears vividly in *Kinshu*, is woman as savior of man. Though the exchange of letters is mutually cathartic, there can be no doubt that the ex-husband, Yasuaki, derives greater benefit from it than the ex-wife, Aki, and that the story may be read, as the critic Hideyuki Sakai notes, as "a tale of [his] salvation through [her]."

The word *kinshū*—a compound of two characters meaning "brocade" and "embroidery"—evokes images that have for centuries been associated with autumnal scenery and poetry, as in the following verse by Ki no Tsurayuki (ca. 872–945):

> *Unseen, in mountain depths the autumn leaves scatter*
> *like brocade under cloak of night.*
> —*Kokinshū* no. 297

While the final scene of the novel beautifully accords with such time-honored poetic allusions, for Miyamoto the metaphor of "brocade" is much broader. In a recent essay, he describes a trip to the autumn mountains and, reflecting on his own illness, he "got the impression that [his] own life was a sort of brocade." Miyamoto's "brocade," then, is also the tapestry of life itself.

It is characteristic of Miyamoto's view of reality that a potentially morbid meditation on life and death is couched in metaphors of great beauty: Mozart's music and brocade.

—Roger K. Thomas